The Needle's Eye

(Revised Edition)

Deanna Nese

Green Avenue Books & Publishing LLC

Paperback Rev. 2nd Ed. 9798330446643

Ebook Rev. 2nd Ed. 9798330446650

Book designed and published by Green Avenue Books & Publishing LLC

Original Publication: iUniverse 2016

For my family.

Contents

<u>1</u>

Mitch

It was summer and Mitch woke up damp and sweaty in the crude shelter he shared with his parents. He'd had the dream again and he desperately wanted to remember it, but even as he strained to recall details, all he visualized was the girl. There was something about her eyes. His nostrils filled with the scent of unwashed people and stale beer. He'd kicked his blanket off during the night and it had landed in a pile of smoldering cigarettes left there by his parents and whoever else was over the night before.

Other people from the encampment were always showing up and would stay late into the night. Last night's details weren't clear to Mitch because he'd recently learned to retreat completely inside his head, which allowed him to tune out much of the unpleasantness around him. This new skill enabled him to listen for the voice, that at the most unexpected times would speak to him, or sometimes give his thoughts a little nudge. The voice was a helpful one and would often lead Mitch where he needed to go.

This morning he was hungry. It had been a week since his parents had brought food home and he wasn't expecting to find much. Mitch spied the red wrapper of a packaged ramen soup poking out from under a tarp. He grabbed an insulated mug and opened it to find only cold, stale coffee. He'd tasted coffee once and found it most unpleasant, hardly worth the trouble, plus it had failed to fill him up or make his stomach stop growling. He settled on the ramen noodles. They tasted pretty good dry, but the seasoning package needed some water or it caused his tongue to sting and made him incredibly thirsty. Luckily, he knew where to find running water. He ran his fingers through his tangled brown hair, grabbed his flip-flops and quietly slipped out, careful not to disturb his parents who were curled up together on a mattress fast asleep.

Mitch walked to a nearby water faucet and not bothering with a cup, he stuck his head directly under the tap and quenched his thirst. He enjoyed the cool water splashing on his face and hair. It was summer, so there was nowhere he had to be. The library, his first choice and usual respite, would not be open for four hours. No one judged him there. It was still early so he knew his parents would sleep for a least a few more hours and since he'd turned nine, he'd been enjoying some new-found freedom in the form of exploring on his own, checking in once in a while and returning home at dark or just after. If asked, he'd tell his parents that he'd been with friends. They wouldn't question him.

Having satisfied his hunger, Mitch considered his options. He knew he didn't want to spend the day at the encampment. It was boring and there was nothing to explore. He began to walk to the temporary vacation campsites just on the other side of the dry river where he and his parents lived. Some brave souls still enjoyed camping as a fun family activity, so there was the possibility of finding kids his age to play with. It helped that in the campground all the children looked dirty and homeless. He may even get fed lunch by their parents. He came to an empty picnic table and stopped to sit. He wanted to hear the voice speak. It didn't. So he wandered. He passed through the campground and encountered no one. He arrived at a chain-link fence. On the other side was a large vacant lot. Mitch had explored the lot before, entering through a small person-sized hole cut into the fencing, but today he climbed right over and dropped into the dry brushy grass.

Anyone driving past would never suspect the magic behind the rusty fence. The large vacant property looked forlorn and forgotten and cautious parents warned their children to stay away. For the adventurous kids who ignored the warnings and went anyway, encounters with angry hornets, prickly burrs or poisonous snakes, encouraged a hasty retreat. Few tried a second time. This allowed the Inside to exist undetected right next to the Outside.

Today Mitch was looking for a sturdy tree to climb, but instead he found a neat looking tunnel in some thick hedges.

He didn't remember seeing it before. His imagination was activated. He hoped the tunnel would lead to a magic land the voice had once spoken of and he had seen in his dreams. Mitch looked up and was startled to observe that the sky had turned an ominous gray. He heard thunder rumble in the distance. There was no choice but to explore, so in he went. He squatted down and crawled through the tunnel on his hands and knees, taking care not to lose a flip-flop, and he arrived in a clearing. Disappointment descended upon him. It looked not a whole lot different from where he'd come. Boring. Until he peeked behind himself and saw the bushes close and the tunnel he'd just passed through, disappear.

"Weird," he thought and was frightened, but not enough to turn back.

There was a path; so he began to follow it. He continued for a while looking down at the dusty ground and trying to make out any footprints. His eyes ached when he raised them, for the sky was a blue he'd never seen before. The gray and thunder from moments before, gone. Mitch came to an interesting fallen tree branch and decided to stop for a moment. It had a perfect hollow place to sit, just his size. He'd lost his sense of time, but figured it was midmorning, and doubted his parents were looking for him. His back fit just right into the nook and it was so comfortable, so peaceful, and the air so breathable, he fell into a light sleep. When he awoke, his cheek was resting on the warm wood. Before he opened his eyes, he felt a presence. He heard the voice that was usually in his head speaking from right beside him, gently calling his name. With a deep breath, he opened his eyes and sitting next to him was a very old man. It was the Sage. The man spoke.

I was wondering when you'd find your way in.

In spite of the fact that he was sitting next to a stranger, a man older than any Mitch had ever seen, he didn't feel afraid. He carefully studied the wizened face, the long white beard, and the gnarled, liver-spotted hands. The man was thin, almost bony and was wearing a frayed beige tunic and pants and worn leather sandals. It may have been a trick of the midmorning light casting shadows in some strange way, but to the boy the old man seemed to be glowing. Mitch found his voice and asked, "Where am I?" and, "Who are you?"

I'm called The Sage and you have found your way Inside.

"Can anyone get in?"

They can and they can't. It depends. It's complicated. But you, I've been expecting.

"Why me?"

I believe you are special.

"Will I be able to go home again? Can I find my way back?"

You have nothing to fear, Mitch. If you don't want to be here, I can make you believe this was a dream and you won't remember a thing. It's up to you.

They sat for a while, and Mitch was surprised but not scared when he realized they were not speaking out loud, but were communicating telepathically. The Sage had been communicating with Mitch for a while and had been hoping he'd figure his way in. If it didn't work out, and on a few other occasions, with other children, it hadn't, the Sage could make the child believe they had merely been dreaming. The memory might nag the child and show up in their drawings, but if they spoke of it, parents were quick to chalk it up to an overactive or even gifted imagination. On the Outside it was accepted and considered normal that children had imaginary friends and believed in imaginary worlds.

The Sage sensed Mitch was a different, special child. He was painfully aware that Mitch had been born to struggling parents who weren't mean people, but were not well equipped to care for themselves, let alone a child. Mitch's parents preferred to live on the fringe of society because they didn't want to belong. They wouldn't take the meds or the compliance pills created to make people peaceful, sedated and willing to obey directions. They had each other and that was enough. But, when Mitch was born, they had no choice but to care for him the best they could.

There had only been a few children, few and far between to the point where the Sage almost stopped hoping that the prophecy would come to pass, thinking that he'd possibly gotten it wrong, or it was still years away before he would be replaced, but here was the boy. That Mitch showed no fear, only curiosity, impressed the Sage.

He found his way in without my help. His eyes looked brown rather than violet, but that could change and it's possible I misunderstood. The rest fit quite nicely, a child finding his way in, able to hear me, and unafraid. Yes, it must be him, but only time will tell.

The Sage took Mitch to the village Inside and showed him around. He introduced him to some of the residents. They greeted him with a reverence and respect unfamiliar, but wholly pleasing to Mitch. He loved it there and felt so comfortable. It was a beautiful, unspoiled paradise to a boy who lived as he did, and when it was time to leave, Mitch was relieved to be promised:

You may come and go whenever you please. You have a safe place here and there is much I wish to teach you.

The Sage held out his hand to Mitch and in it was a small wooden ring.

If you put this on your finger, I'll always be able to find you, and you'll always be able to get back Inside.

"I'll be back. I'll be back whenever I can," Mitch replied. That night he slept soundly for the first time in a long time and he looked forward to the days of summer ahead of him. He briefly considered telling his parents of his discovery, but something held him back.

Fitting in at school had always been a struggle for Mitch. He was dirty and often hungry and embarrassed of his growling stomach, which made it challenging to focus during lessons. He tried his best to blend into the background and was virtually friendless, close to no one. If you didn't have a real home to live in, you couldn't have friends over to play. If you could never invite anyone, they would never invite you either, and so it went. Even the birthday parties where the entire class was invited, Mitch could not attend. He wouldn't dream of asking his parents permission and of course having a gift for the birthday child was not possible.

So, he took sanctuary Inside after he discovered it, which is what made his childhood bearable. As long as he was back at his parents' shelter by dark, he wasn't missed. He came and went frequently over the next few years, unnoticed on the Outside and welcomed on the Inside. There were times he considered staying permanently, but he couldn't. His parents could never get Inside, of this he felt inexplicably certain. And even though on a daily basis Mitch's emotions regarding his parents ran the gamut from gut love to contempt and feverish dislike, he wasn't ready to leave them behind forever.

<u>2</u>

Eden

Mitch had found 'Inside' easily as a child because he was young and alone and he needed to. At age fourteen, a full year earlier than most, Mitch applied and was accepted to the Upper School for Adolescents (U.S.A.). He chose to live in the dorms with the other commoner kids and he focused all his attention on his studies. He was quiet and still had no close friends. He often longed for the peace and comfort of Inside, but he never went. There were even times he thought he'd imagined the whole experience as a way to deal with his rough childhood, but then he looked at his ring and knew for certain he hadn't imagined it.

It wasn't until he found himself alone at nineteen, with nothing but his thoughts and his infant girl, Eden, that he began to seek the world he'd known as a boy, the Inside.

For his entire life, Mitch and his parents had been homeless, and it had taken its toll. Mitch had distanced himself out of self-preservation years before, but he never lived too far away. Out of respect or pride, his father never asked for help, but Mitch gave him money when he could and tried his best to get both his parents into recovery programs. They politely declined every offer. As for his mother, a drug overdose took her suddenly, and when Mitch was asked to identify the body at the morgue, he hardly recognized her. Soon after, Mitch's father, Joe, took his own life. To him the world had become unbearable and there seemed no possible respite, no reason to continue living after losing his wife, his only love.

The night Mitch received the news about his mother's death, he was staying up late in his cramped apartment, working on his research which involved examining the effects on children of childhood neglect. He had just downed his third cup of coffee and eaten his fifth piece of pepperoni pizza with ghost peppers, his usual writing menu. Shame flooded over him along with the guilt of wondering if there was any way he could have fixed his parents or helped them, at the very least. Then the call he had been dreading, came. It was the news he'd been expecting and preparing for all his life.

"Yes, that's her, she's my mother, Edith Allbright."

His mother looked so old on the metal gurney. Deep lines filled with dirt ridged her face and she looked as though no amount of showering could ever make her clean. Her hair was thin, gray, and matted, her clothes stiff with dirt. The smell of urine emanated from her. The soles of her shoes were worn thin and her socks appeared to have grown into the scabby skin on her thin shins. She was 39 years old, only 20 years older than Mitch, but she looked ancient. How could she have fallen so far? Why was he not enough to save her, to make her want to be a better person? Upon seeing his mother, he was filled with grief, but behind the grief was something else, an enormous sense of relief and determination. He had escaped the life he could have been destined for.

The best way to honor his parents was to become an advocate for children who were suffering now as he had as a child, and to protect little Eden. It was then he knew. He needed to bring Eden Inside where she could be safe and protected. And he did. And she was. Being only about six months, Mitch believed she was too young to have any memory of her brief time Outside.

So the little girl grew up and thrived Inside, in the protected space, raised by all the women collectively, and without the chaos and distractions of the Outside world. She never had a day when she didn't feel surrounded by love, she knew nothing else. Still, as she grew, Eden became curious about the Outside. She knew her father worked there and she wanted to go with him. Mitch wanted nothing more than to protect her and keep her safe Inside.

Few who lived life safely Inside ever wanted or chose to leave. Why would they? Occasionally someone went out for a few years of Outside Experience and Education, to better understand the world and serve newcomers who needed them, but certainly never any as young as Eden. Everyone knew at age nineteen they must decide which world to stay in.

After the age of nineteen, all persons must choose which world to belong to. You can't exist in both.

Mitch worried about Eden being exposed to a world so different than the only one she knew. He was grateful he'd found the place once again that had so comforted him as a child, and thankful, he'd found it when he needed it the most.

Only I knew better. Part of me wanted to warn Mitch, but I knew I couldn't.

After years of peace Inside, everyone was aware, though no one wanted to dwell on it. A threat to the Inside loomed. One day there would be a betrayal. The Sage spoke of it and everyone knew it was part of the prophecy. Realizing this, the Sage wished to keep Eden Inside. He hoped that she might be one of the few to never venture out, to spend a lifetime living in this protected world, continuing her Pure Heart training, knowing once she left, temptation would be introduced.

We are to be ever vigilant. We know not when or from where this threat will come, but it will come.

<u>3</u>

Going Outside

The first time she left, Eden was only nine and small for her age at that. Her mind and her curiosity made her seem much older. Mitch wondered if it was possible some part of her remembered her brief time spent Outside as an infant. Most children never asked about the Outside, and most never tried to do things differently, only Eden.

"Dad please. I want to go with you. I want to see the other world. I need to see if it's how I imagine. Let me go once, then I promise not to bug you. I'll never ask again," and Eden looked at her father with those violet eyes. To her it was like being pulled by a force not in her control. She was compelled to beg her father relentlessly. Her only experience different from the one she lived was through the classical books she so avidly devoured, and the pictures created so vividly in her mind.

Eden was aware that her dad was concerned and troubled by her request to go out. He knew what lurked Outside and wanted nothing more than to protect her. But he finally gave in.

Looking back years later, Eden would recall everything in sharp detail from that first day she went Outside. The day before her excursion, she and her father went to Clothing. Clothing was sandwiched between Supplies and Books. The difference between Clothing and a thrift store Outside is that all the garments in Clothing are beige, or neutral with no embellishments, just simple, comfortable and roomy. Eden and her father searched the racks until the woman in charge suggested they look in the back closet for something more suitable. There Eden found the colors and patterns.

It strained her eyes to see printed on fabric what she had only observed in nature before, the patterns, the colors, and the sheer variety. Eden tried on the clothes and for the very first time, saw her reflection in a full-length mirror. She liked what she saw. She brought her hand to her face and caressed it. She touched and flipped her long golden hair. She focused on her own eyes. They, too, were a color she had never seen in nature and she was mesmerized. For the first time, she really saw what she looked like.

"Dad look at me," Eden said, "I'm beautiful."

"Of course you are, Sweetie. Don't I tell you every day?" Mitch answered.

A simple dress of deep blue was chosen for Eden, and a single ribbon for her hair. Just putting the clothes on her body increased the pull she felt to get out and experience the other side, the Outside. Eden wondered if her dad had refused her, if she'd never asked, if it would have been different. Later, she knew the answer, but she wouldn't change her decision. The future was bound to happen, one way or another.

On the day Eden first ventured out, it was only after much deliberation and quiet meetings between Mitch and the Sage. Eden would be able to come back in, of course, and she would be with her father, a respected member of the community, practically the Sage's apprentice, who could freely travel between Inside and Outside. Thus, it was determined safe enough.

Eden listened in as the Sage spoke with her father, weighing the options. She heard him say, "If we let the Inside-borns leave too early, our community might lose them. It's too risky to send you to try to fetch them. Send a parent, and that parent will never get back Inside. I don't think children are equipped to navigate the Outside on their own."

Eden, an avid reader of many books, had constructed detailed images of what she would encounter Outside. She wanted to see crowds and colors. Above all, she wanted to see the difference. Knowing this and wishing to help satisfy her curiosity, the Sage took Eden and her father to a parking garage elevator which exited onto a busy street. It was one of the many exit/entrance points connecting the worlds.

Mitch watched his little daughter touch the walls and close her eyes. The walls were scratched up with messages etched into them by bored people wanting to leave their mark. The elevator lurched to a stop and the heavy door slid open. Clutching hands, the two made their way onto the busy street. Eden covered her ears as it seemed noise and sounds were assaulting her from every direction. An understanding dawned on her.

"Dad, it's so loud," she shouted. "Is this why the Fallen need quiet?"

"Yes, exactly," Mitch said.

The noise was almost too much, too overwhelming. Her eyes stung and were tearing up. She clung to her dad. Her small freckled nose crinkled, taking in the strange and unfamiliar smells. They walked on dirty pavement littered with trash blowing in little swirls around their feet. Wads of gum seemed to be plastered on every surface. The air smelled and tasted so different here. It was heavy and layered with scents of rotting garbage, exhaust fumes, food and people. Eden could detect no freshness at all. She could almost feel her lungs filling with particles too minute to see, not quite able to fully expand. When she looked to the sky, she saw no blue, just a dim cloudless gray and layers of brown. Eden felt sad for the lack of beauty here. So far, it was nothing like she had hoped.

"I want to see pretty things, are there any?" Eden asked.

A desperate group of pigeons pecked at invisible grains on the sidewalk and a few feet away lay a pigeon alone. It was not moving. The breeze was blowing the feathers on the bird's spine backwards. Mitch fixed Eden with sad eyes, "It's dead," and when she went to touch it, he gently pulled her away, sorry that she'd seen it.

"We should bury it properly," Eden stated. It was clear she was upset, but Mitch frowned.

"No, that's not what they do here."

This troubled Eden. She wondered if anyone would notice the bird, or care? Would the bird move on as people do, or would he come back again as a bird or another creature? Eden pulled away for a brief second, and reached out to touch the creature gently with just the tip of one finger before moving on. She saw its wing flutter. She said nothing to her dad as she watched the bird rise and fly away.

"It's not good for us to be out in this air." Mitch tugged her along leading them to the enclosed catwalks that crisscrossed the city center where the air was filtered through giant machines vibrating with a constant hum. Eden pondered what it would be like, if the giant machines shut off and which was worse, the ever-present noise pollution or the poor quality of the air without them?

She and her dad would take the public speed train to the school where Mitch worked trying his best to save young ones, children identified as "troubled." Eden longed to explore the streets more, but it was important to stay within the enclosures, especially in this part of the city. Trains were speeding in both directions with such force it frightened her, but she never let on. She stood tall and bravely, trying to appear like she'd been here, done this many times before, grateful for the reassuring grip of her dad's hand. Her face did not betray her and Mitch was impressed by her calm demeanor, as she gazed expectantly with those violet eyes so different from his own. She looked ready for adventure.

On the train, people looked down and stared at their devices whether they were standing or sitting. Almost everyone had some type of food or drink, which was odd. Inside, people only ate or drank in the common hall at the same time as everyone else. Eden's sense of smell felt overwhelmed again. Mitch was used to it. Some scents were unpleasant, but not all. A man near them had a ball of bread with a shine on it that smelled sweet and positively heavenly. Eden's mouth watered. She wanted a bite.

"What is he eating?" she whispered.

"It's a donut. Maybe I'll take you to try one later. It might be fun to taste something off the standard menu. Would you like that?" Mitch asked.

Everything Eden ate was grown and made Inside, but she had heard about restaurants and exotic foods, a snippet here and there mostly from her skills at Spying and Reporting. She was intrigued. Her dad turned to her and said, "Ask me anything, I know there are a million questions in that pretty head of yours."

Her questions tumbled out with no filter.

"Why does nobody talk to us?"

"Eden, they don't know us here. People on the Outside don't usually speak to others they don't know. They're private. Their minds are occupied."

"Is it always so crowded?"

"Yes, it feels that way, crowded, but lonely since hardly anyone talks to each other. You would think that it would be tiring trying to keep up with everyone, but people's worlds are small here, they only see what they want to see."

"The sky, it's not blue. Why is that?" Eden thought she knew the answer before she asked and it saddened her.

"It's been poisoned. If the people here want to see blue sky, they do it virtually, through a program. If you want to see blue skies in nature, it's really expensive. It costs a lot of money."

"Where are all the people going, and why do they hurry?" She wanted to know. Mitch informed her.

"Most people have jobs, like you've read about in books, and they pay close attention to time here."

They continued on to his job site where he worked as a counselor. Mitch hadn't spoken often to Eden about what he did Outside; it was a part of his life she knew very little of. He struggled to fill in a few gaps before they arrived at the Lower School for children ages six to fourteen.

"Honey, you know how Inside you go to training with some other kids your age and you have your duties, and when you are ready you learn to read and then you choose for yourself whatever it is you want to learn; you just go to Books and pick up anything and you feel what's right? Well, in this world, children go to Lower School from ages six to fourteen and they all learn the same things, the same subjects. They don't choose. That doesn't happen until Upper School and there are still not many choices even then. In fact, they really don't choose at all until they specialize, if they get that far. If they don't, they work."

It all sounded pretty awful even as he was trying to make it seem natural, just completely different from what she knew. He had no idea how much detail to give or even if Eden needed any at all. Her intuition was sharp but Mitch feared that the realities here would frighten or confuse her. He began to second guess whether she should have been allowed out, but he knew if there was a real danger, the Sage would not have sanctioned it.

The Sage sensed Eden was destined to leave. If not now, then soon. Few spoken words passed between Mitch and the Sage. Their communication was telepathic and had been since before Mitch had ever met him face to face. Both felt confident Mitch would be the successor to the Sage, when the time was right and the prophecy fulfilled.

Eden continued asking questions.

"Can I meet some friends here?"

"I don't think so. It wouldn't be wise, Sweetie. The children are different. They don't get Pure Heart Training. Some are naturally good, but others are mean-spirited and might want to hurt you. I couldn't bear it, Eden. It's so hard to be a child here. It was miserable for me. The only thing that got me through was the Sage and discovering the Inside. If I hadn't, I don't know what I would have become."

"If you don't like it here, why do you come out?" It was an insightful question to ask.

"It's my duty. I need to go between the worlds. It's hard to explain, but the Sage and I believe a threat is imminent. It's coming. One of the worlds is threatened and may soon cease to exist. We aren't sure which one, but we think the key to the survival of both worlds is through the children."

"Will you be sad if I leave Inside when I am old enough?"

Eden knew the answer, but wanted to hear it anyway.

"Yes, but I know you'll find your own way. When you practice being 'quiet,' I think you'll know where you're supposed to be." Mitch gave her a gentle hug.

"One more thing Eden, before I forget. Remember not to speak about the Inside today. People here won't understand."

"Okay, Dad. I'll remember."

Eden asked even more questions that day, as she always did, and Mitch answered with his patient and understanding way, in his calm and even tone.

They exited the train at Upper School rather than Lower and decided to walk through that campus. The halls were empty and eerily silent, the linoleum floor brilliantly shiny without any scuff marks. There were hundreds of clear, stacked boxes built into the walls on either side. Most were empty.

"Lockers," Mitch pointed. "It's where the students put their personal belongings." The doors were closed all along the hall except for one. Eden peeked in and when she did, saw teenagers, all with headsets, seated in rows staring ahead at some invisible scene only they could see.

"It's not time for Conversation," said Mitch. "These students are learning their specialties." To Eden it looked boring just sitting there staring and she wondered if the dream of going to school Outside when she was older was a good idea, but Mitch assured her this was only part of the day. Time would also be spent in Conversation and Discussion as well as Physical Activity, to keep the body healthy.

They finally made it to the Lower School where Mitch conducted his counseling groups and sessions with troubled youth. Eden hadn't thought much about boys yet; they were part of the scenery Inside along with anyone else. She considered them decent playmates and found they were often more willing than girls to participate in some of her more creative games that skirted the rules, like "Spy and Report." This was a game that involved exactly what it sounds like. Eden and her friends would listen to adults undetected, learning things they suspected were meant to be private and not for their ears.

The boys Eden roped into her schemes were reluctant accomplices, and even more so when they were called out by the Sage and reprimanded. Eden, on the other hand, was never called out which made her wonder if the Sage couldn't read her and wasn't able to hear her thoughts. The Sage's intuition was spot-on with most people, but the majority were neither prone to, nor interested in, stirring up trouble. Eden knew it was wrong and against the edicts, but dragging others into her mischief brought her great satisfaction. It was a challenge. In her bed in the dead of night, remorse would creep its way into her heart, but never enough to stop her from testing the limits time and time again.

Nearing his classroom, Mitch expressly directed her.

"I need you to obey me today. This is important, Eden. Do you understand?" As a dad, Mitch tended toward indulgence. He believed in allowing Eden to explore and make her own way as much as possible and he was even willing to cover for her when she made some poor choices. He always exhibited patience. It was the essence of his nature.

"I'll be working with a group of kids who need my help. You'll wait for me with Marie," Mitch explained. Not getting why she couldn't be included, but also wanting to show that she could follow directions and not be a nuisance, that she wouldn't be any trouble at all, Eden said only, "Fine."

Before the session, they walked over to Marie's office, where Eden was to stay until Mitch came back for her. Marie had an open, friendly face and Eden half-listened as she introduced herself and extended her hand. Eden shook it firmly.

"It's nice to meet you," she said. Then she stood by her father and waited.

"Mitch, I don't know what it is, but I feel really sick." Marie's face went pale and slick with perspiration as they stood there, and she ran, bent over, arms hugging her middle, the painful cramps coming out of nowhere. Mitch called after her.

"No worries, Marie. Feel better. I'll take Eden with me."

The guilt Eden felt was minimal. She'd caused discomfort and some pain, nothing too serious. In her opinion, she did what she had to do. When was she ever going to get the chance to be with Outside kids? In her dad's eyes Eden thought she detected an ever-slight suspicion, but left with no other alternative, Mitch had to take her along. If he was able to read Eden, he certainly never let on that there was anything unusual about her, anything different.

So he told her firmly, "When I'm working with the students, you must sit quietly, Eden, you mustn't speak."

For the day's session, there would be just four boys. The small group met three days a week and the focus was managing anger. Anger was a foreign emotion to Eden. She'd seldom witnessed it or any other extreme emotions firsthand. Inside, people take care to use quiet voices and to practice sensitivity, not to speak unless approached. From a young age Insiders learn to read others by their eyes. People speak softly, soothingly.

Mitch's biggest concern was the youngest boy, Sterling. This little guy was a bomb ready to detonate. He was offensive, unruly and had no friends. Other kids feared him. Every year the boy's instructors referred him to Mitch and Mitch worked with him as best he could. Sterling's teachers had been spit on, cursed at, and punched. One new teacher cried as she told Mitch, the ever-patient counselor, she was afraid of the boy, afraid of those black, dead eyes that seemed to register no emotion except anger and something more sinister.

When concerns were brought to his parents' attention, they laughed it off claiming, "Boys will be boys." Occasionally Sterling's parents would threaten to take him out of Lower School, but they never followed through. Mitch believed they cherished the six-hour break school provided them. It was certainly a break for the boy's nanny who suffered relentlessly from his constant abuse. By all accounts Sterling was a beautiful boy, with the exception of those haunted, hollow eyes.

As Mitch had explained to Eden, there were few choices for schooling Outside and strict adherence was required. Being unable to control one's anger was a problem requiring a fix or these boys would not progress.

When Mitch told Eden the children he worked with were troubled, she thought immediately of Vita, her closest friend and ally. Vita was beginning to draw away from Eden, to distance herself. Some of Eden's ideas made her friend uncomfortable. Recently Vita had threatened to go to the Sage, not to get Eden in trouble, it was only out of concern and Vita's compulsion to follow the edict: "We must help first." Eden didn't consider herself troubled, only different, but she wondered if the label fit her, too.

Filled with anticipation, Eden followed her father into the counseling room. She was thrilled at the chance to see some troubled kids up close. The room was small, about half the size of the classrooms off the lodge. It was quiet. Walls were a blue that the sky here should be, but wasn't. "Nice touch, Dad." Eden thought. Puffy floor chairs that Mitch called bean bags were piled on a plush rug in the center of the room and they begged to be touched. Eden was distracted by the rug as she made her way to the corner by her dad's desk, but she was determined to follow his directions.

"You need to stay over here, Eden." He pointed to where he had pulled an armchair behind the desk and set out some colored pencils and drawing sheets to occupy her. It was not to be. She didn't plan to disobey. She didn't plan to meddle. She watched three boys enter, and then came Sterling, followed by a large man in an all blue uniform. Sterling's eyes were downcast, his shoulders bent. He oozed defiance. Eden popped out of the chair and made a beeline straight to him. Her dad tried to intercept what he was sure would be a blow to the face, but he wasn't fast enough.

Eden held out her hand. She had no fear of this boy, the most troubled kid Lower School had seen in anyone's recent memory, and she introduced herself.

"I'm Eden. And you are?"

"Sterling," came the reply in an even, almost shy tone.

Having narrowly avoided disaster, Mitch realized he was holding his breath and he released it in a long sigh.

"Eden, please sit at my desk," he calmly and firmly reminded, desperately trying to send her a signal of warning. Hearing this, Sterling balled up his fists, a sure sign he was about to lose control. He spoke directly to Mitch, "Please, Mr. Mitch, can she please stay here?"

"Okay."

Mitch let her. He could never have explained why.

"Come sit with me," Sterling commanded while pulling her somewhat forcefully toward him. Eden knew nothing of his background, but it would not have mattered if she had. Those black, black eyes, long feathery eyelashes, and perfect olive skin. Eden was not too young to be struck by Sterling's beauty. It was hard to believe he was real and there is no other explanation than to say she felt a connection, felt that finally in her world, there was another like her.

Eden sat right next to Sterling and respectfully listened to the other boys as they shared their highs and lows of the week. On this day, Sterling decided to share. It was a rarity for him to participate.

"Okay, so my 'low' for the week was when I pushed Marcus. I broke his tablet, too. I shattered the screen. He bawled like a big baby."

None of the other boys looked surprised.

"I guess my 'high point' was just today. I made a friend. Her name is Eden," and Sterling smiled, a real smile.

After that day, Eden wouldn't remember the names or faces of the other boys present. None interested her but Sterling.

"I'll see you next session," he said with a grin and a bounce on his feet.

"No, I'm only here today. I won't see you again," Eden responded, sounding disappointed.

Sterling issued a deep guttural sound, grabbed the closest object, a bean bag, and hurled it at the closest person, another boy, who responded in kind with a sharp punch to Sterling's chest. Eden watched fascinated as the two boys rolled on the floor, fists flying. Then she commanded, "Dad, make them stop!"

"That's your second infraction this week Sterling, you're coming with me." The large man in all blue began to escort him from the room. Sterling crumpled his body and let himself be dragged.

"I'll send you a note with my dad," Eden shouted and they locked eyes.

<u>4</u>

Sterling

Sterling had always been untouchable, born to wealthy parents who kept up appearances and placed the utmost importance on protocol. Every move and decision his parents made was designed to create the illusion of perfection. They had even created Sterling himself in a lab, separating the good genes from the less desired ones and adding a few. Genes were selected for physical appearance including height. He would be six foot three as an adult. He would have dark brown, thick hair and he would never experience baldness. He would have olive skin that wouldn't burn in the sun, only tan. The selections would mean he would not need any plastic surgery until he was older, at least late 20's. Genes for cancer were weeded out. Genes for high intelligence, selected. Though dark green eyes were chosen with 20/20 lifetime vision, Sterling was born with dark, almost black eyes.

The program was not always one hundred percent accurate. The technology was cutting edge and some people were frightened by it. It was mainly the rich using it in secret to create beautiful and perfect offspring, but they didn't want to brag even to each other, because it was still new and a little taboo, so best to let everyone think that your perfect child was a gift of your own perfect heritage, if you were lucky enough to conceive a child at all.

By the time Sterling was born, his parents barely spoke to one another. He was indeed a beautiful baby, loved in the capacity his parents were capable of, and spoiled. Great care was taken to choose a nanny that was pretty, but not too pretty, someone who could blend into the background and not cause a stir, not too old, not too young, experienced, but moldable. The nanny's uniform was plain pants or a beige skirt with a light-colored, collared shirt and plain shoes. The nanny's job was to keep Sterling safe and happy without ever uttering the word, "No." Nanny was to anticipate his every possible want or need and fulfill it.

Sterling was never to be denied anything, never to feel left out. Well, this soon instilled a sense of entitlement rivaling any royal born prince and presented no small challenge to a caregiver. Not to mention, the job required fast and creative thinking to keep a boy whose mission in life was to stir up trouble from stirring up trouble. Poor Sterling had no concept of the real world and was shocked, bewildered and more than a little nasty when something didn't go his way, because his experiences were manipulated to always go his way. He treated his nanny with rude remarks, constantly trying to get a rise out of her, desperately wanting to provoke her, and cause a reaction besides the constant boring sameness he'd grown accustomed to. During Sterling's formative years there were many nannies because of this; they were all called "Nanny" and the sameness made it challenging to tell one from another. The job paid well, but not well enough.

It was at a friend's house, actually a classmate's, when Sterling first experienced the concept of No. The boys had made a rather large mess of the playroom and had become bored with each other's company. At that point, Sterling decided he wanted candy.

"I'll have candy now."

He was told No by his playmate's mother.

"It is not allowed before dinner, and you boys need to clean this mess."

"But I'm allowed!" Sterling blurted and was promptly countered with, "Not in this house, you're not."

So he demanded to leave. The nanny was called. She cleaned up the mess they'd made of the playroom while the boy shot daggers at her with his eyes, and then sulked indignantly all the way home where he could gorge on candy, skip dinner altogether, and play video games, before falling into a fitful sleep. This was the very first time Sterling felt truly displeased with his situation. He was nine.

<u>5</u>

No Turning Back

The evening of the day she'd gone out, Eden was positively buzzing with energy and excitement.

"Dad, I want to go every week. You can take me with you. I want to see more. I want to see Sterling."

Mitch feared for her, as did the Sage. There was no going back. Had she seen too much, too soon? Her small world had expanded and she was filled with questions.

At his house that evening Sterling approached his parents.

"I've made a friend."

Both parents sipped drinks, not bothering to raise their eyes, distractedly flicking the screens on their devices. Sterling threw a plate. It smashed on the wall narrowly missing their heads.

"Oh, dear!"

The nanny scuttled over and began to pick up the larger pieces.

"You what now, Son?"

Mr. Silver gave a sideways glance, one eye still fixed on the screen, but from his mother, nothing at all.

"Never mind!" Sterling shouted and stormed to his room where he could punch his pillow and cry privately.

True to her word, Eden sent a note to Sterling via her father, and Sterling responded. The letters traveled back and forth on a regular basis, sometimes daily. It would have been easy for Mitch to open and read the crudely sealed envelopes, but he resisted, respecting Eden's privacy. In her letters Eden requested such things as, "Tell me more about how you got in trouble this week. How did you steal from the other boy? Did he cry? Did you get away with it? What is your house like? Tell me more about the food."

Sterling's inquiries were telling too, but not to Eden. He wanted to know about life Inside, every detail. He didn't know how to phrase his questions, but the Sage knew and could read between the lines. Sterling wanted to try out not being angry, not fighting, just being calm. Eventually, as the Sage knew he would, Mitch came to him.

"I want to bring a boy in. I think we can make a difference. He is trying to be good. He needs this." His concern for Eden was written on his face.

As anyone could see, Eden was looking thin. Dark rings rimmed her eyes, her skin was sallow, but she was not ill.

"Eden, I was thinking. What if I brought Sterling here for a visit? Would that make you happy?" The words were out before Mitch could mentally explore possible consequences, and once they were, Eden's life-spark returned.

"Of course it depends on the Sage's approval", he added quickly, knowing there was no real need to ask. The Sage's trust in him was absolute. He was only trying to create an out if he should change his mind.

And so, Mitch decided that both children would benefit if Sterling came in. Eden's curiosity at least for now would be satisfied and as for Sterling, well, Sterling could use any positive influence he could get. The poor kid was a mess and so angry he was widely considered a lost cause among those who worked with him, except Mitch. For some reason he couldn't put into words, Mitch had a soft spot for this boy.

<u>6</u>

Going Inside

Mitch sought permission from Sterling's parents to take the boy off-campus. He called them in for a meeting at the school. They seemed annoyed to have to attend and the large man in the tight-fitting suit asked Mitch to please make it quick and get to the point. The woman signed off without a word. She seemed impatient and eager to leave. It was all Mitch could do not to chuckle out loud as the image of a quaking Chihuahua alongside a lumbering, overweight bulldog came to mind. He hid a laugh behind a cough as the strange couple officially granted permission for their son to take part in the therapy.

"Now if that's all, we'll be on our way. I'm a very busy man, I'll have you know." Mr. and Mrs. Silver stood to leave.

As part of the therapy process, Sterling would be taken on a series of field trips during the day. He would travel off campus under Mitch's supervision. Mitch shifted part of his caseload to his colleagues to make the accommodation. To Sterling he explained, "We are going to take a hike through an old camp ground."

Outside kids found it amusing that years before, people would sleep outside for fun, as a vacation. But the Earth's temperature had risen so dramatically, so rapidly, that being out in the air for any length of time these days was considered dangerous and ill-advised. This is what made it so exciting for kids, who cared little about the possible health damage.

"You're going to have to behave. No tantrums. No questions. This was a special place for me when I was about your age. I'm going to show you a place that very few people know about and very few will ever visit. You're going to have to trust me and even though secrets are not usually a good thing, I'm going to ask you to keep what you see a secret."

"Are you taking me Inside?" Sterling asked.

"So Eden had told him, but how much?" Mitch wondered.

"Is this the place where Eden lives? I will behave. I want to go."

Mitch planned to take Sterling through the same entrance he'd discovered as a boy. He rarely used it now. It had been years, in fact, and he wondered if it was still there. No one occupied the old campground any more, and the two passed through to the vacant lot. The fence separating the two areas had long since been flattened. The entire area appeared abandoned, not having yet been developed and covered. Mitch wondered how long it would remain so.

Big real estate companies were slowly buying properties like these and trying to recreate a natural area under a protective dome. As the cities expanded, the land might be subsumed into the vast network of tubes and tunnels and air filtration systems. At present it looked much the same as when Mitch was a boy, but he doubted anyone still lived here out in the elements as his parents had.

Walking through the old grounds, he was overtaken by nostalgia. Rough as his life had been, he'd had freedom to explore and touch nature. So sad, most of today's kids who lived Outside, would never experience the world Mitch knew as a child. The memory of this beauty, while preserved forever in programs, would soon be forgotten in the minds of the people. On screen things looked as brilliant as they used to, but here in real time it was as if the entire area had been painted over in sepia tones, giving everything a dull, brownish wash.

Sterling was taking his time, walking slowly a few paces behind Mitch. He had kicked off his sneakers and socks instinctively, throwing them over a shoulder where they bumped his back with each step. The terrain was rough, but Mitch was certain no harm would come to the boy. Sterling chose a rock, carefully weighing it, and then throwing it with all his might. It landed with a satisfying thud and a smile played on his lips as he looked at Mitch, who nodded his approval, grabbing a rock of his own and hurling it into the distance. Further on, the hedge Mitch recognized from his boyhood appeared.

"Here's the place."

As they touched the leaves, branches parted and the familiar tunnel appeared. They crouched down.

"You first," Mitch said, as Sterling pushed through, eager to see what awaited him. Mitch followed close behind. Sterling stood and gazed, momentarily stunned.

"I feel like I'm in the screen, except this is better than Eden described it."

A hawk swooped. A breeze blew gently across Sterling's face. Rabbits scurried in underbrush.

As if on cue, Eden appeared. She spotted Sterling and rushed right over, throwing her arms around Sterling without a moment's hesitation.

"Why are you not in class? I was going to come and find you," Mitch said. He wasn't upset, but marveled at Eden's perceptiveness. How did she know to appear at the exact moment?

The pair took off with Mitch's permission and a promise to meet at the common hall for the midday meal. Eden found joy in showing her friend what she most loved in her community. They swung from a rope and landed in the creek, soaking wet and laughing. For a good fifteen minutes the two watched a mother bird care for her babies in a nest.

"This doesn't seem real," Sterling marveled.

"How are we this close to a bird? I usually shoot them in my games, but this is so much better."

It startled him to realize that even if he had a gun right then, he would not shoot the bird. Eden taught him to pile rocks. They began with the largest and most stable, slowly adding more while paying attention to the delicate balance. When the towers would tumble, Sterling gathered the stones and patiently tried again to achieve the perfect balance, enjoying the challenge. He recalled a similar game he'd once played, but instead of enjoyment, he'd been frustrated and lashed out at another kid, resulting in a punishment. He didn't feel his usual frustration and anger with Eden.

"What do you call this?" Sterling wrapped his arms around himself. "My chest hurts."

Eden responded knowingly, "It's joy. It's happiness. I feel it too."

The children looked up. The sky Inside was always a dazzling azure, but now clouds obscured the sun and blue changed to a fierce and angry gray while a low rumble was felt more than heard.

"I wanted you to see the blue sky in real life, like I wrote to you about. I'm not sure what's happening to it today." A storm brewed inside the clouds and for some it was peculiar and unnerving to see the always-blue sky turn. The temperature dipped below the usual threshold of 70 degrees, and Eden and Sterling began to shiver.

"I think we better get to the hall. It's almost time for the midday meal." Eden was eager to show Sterling more of her world, but nervous about sharing him with anyone else. They entered the hall a few minutes late. The crowds gathered at the long wooden tables. People seemed edgy and were speaking in low tones about the weather.

Sterling, enthralled, strained to catch a snippet of what they were saying. All he could make out were fragments of conversation.

"I don't like this. It makes me uneasy. I've never seen the sky gray Inside. I've never heard thunder Inside."

"Do you think it's a sign?"

"A sign of what?" Sterling wondered.

Today it felt like the entire Inside population was present, about 140 at any given time. Eden and Sterling squeezed in next to Eden's friend Vita, and Eden whispered a quick introduction. Unable as usual to adhere to the edict of quiet reflection before meals, Eden continued to ask questions in her best quiet voice.

"What's with the crowd? What's going on today?"

Vita, ever patient with her friend, mumbled under her breath, "The Exit."

Then Eden remembered. Five would leave today, two men, and three women. Their training complete, it was time to go back out and serve. They had come in as Fallens, no longer able to function in the Outside world, ready to leave it permanently. It was Sterling's turn to whisper, "Who is that?" He was staring at the Sage. He'd never seen a man so old with so many wrinkles. To Sterling, he looked ancient.

"He's the Sage, I'll introduce you later, he's in charge here," she paused. "But, he's good. Everyone loves the Sage. You will too, I promise."

Each person who would exit that day stepped up, giving a brief speech mentioning how he or she would take what they learned Inside to help heal the Outside in any small way they could. Each also explained their choice of where they would work Outside, where they felt they could best contribute. The Sage attended but spoke little during these ceremonies except to remind the newest ambassadors:

Everything counts.

Let everything you do be for the greater good. Harm no one. Help whenever you can. No act is too small. Stay away from that which tempts you, and if you do this, you will move forward.

It was a tall order. They had come in as Fallens, ready to end their lives, and were leaving with hope to help change others and to stick around until their own lives ended naturally and they could move forward. The Sage had positive feelings about this group and doubted any would fall again. He reminded them to never remove their rings. This would allow him to be connected to them when they went out, to watch their lives as they progressed. It gave the Sage great satisfaction to see the Ambassadors out in the world. It was clear he considered them his own children.

As he watched and listened, Sterling was confused and troubled. Afterward, he asked Mitch, "What did that lady mean when she said she was going to work with the abandoned children?"

Mitch responded with carefully chosen words, unsure how much or how little Sterling knew and keenly aware of the fragile balance in the boy between anger and calm. This was no place for one of his infamous outbursts.

"Not all children have parents."

The confused expression on Sterling's face revealed he was not aware of this.

Mitch continued. "It's not a crime to not want your child and some people just turn them in. It's allowed up to the age of five with no questions asked." Explaining this reality was particularly hard for Mitch. His own parents had kept him despite the challenge it posed, and yet others were able to walk away from their babies. Try as he might, he would never really understand.

"So some kids are taken in and cared for by other people. Is that right?" Sterling asked.

"Yes, that's right," Eden chimed in impatiently. "I mean it's not really a big deal. They have a place to live and everything." This was true, but Mitch thought children needed more and deserved better.

Two of the women exiting today would work with these children trying to provide what the children's own parents could not or would not. A few might be brought Inside by Mitch himself, but most would live in dorm-like facilities where their basic necessities would be taken care of. Then they'd be groomed for a life of service to the general population performing the tasks and jobs deemed beneath members of upper society. A select few would be allowed higher education. It was a flawed system, Mitch knew, yet he could not deny in many ways things were actually better than in times past.

Most of the people he dealt with who served the larger population seemed content with their station. Still, he knew few would ever have children of their own and he felt it unfair. Major corruption still flourished at the top, but at least some humanitarian efforts were now being made for those on the bottom in this caste-like system.

The other three leaving today would work in H.R. (Homeless Residence) likely in the area of counseling and mental health. Outside, the homeless problem is considered solved. There are warehouses with heating in winter, cooling in summer, and beds and meals provided, but in order to take advantage of these places, one must be willing to submit to the meds. The meds are designed to make people peaceful, compliant, sedated and willing to obey directions and complete whatever job is assigned to them.

It seemed no one ever chose to work in the Environmental Division any more. A choice once popular, these days it was rarely picked, the Outside so damaged, few Ambassadors believed they could make an appreciable difference, and the more time passed, the less people cared to have things back the way they were. Living in virtual reality was the new normal. One need never leave the enclosures to venture outside into the air at all, especially if they are wealthy. It's possible to program anything you like and to feel as if you are there bodily experiencing everything, the sounds, touch, and tastes.

The new Ambassadors seemed ready for the challenges they would face, and all Inside wished them well. After the midday meal, Eden showed Sterling where she lived with her dad.

"It's really just where we sleep." The small wooden framed burre was simple. They took three steps up into a large room divided into two sleeping areas, and in the center, a simple fireplace and a lamp with two comfortable chairs. The structure was surrounded by a small narrow deck. The restroom and showers were central in a little courtyard and shared by six other little burres. People had few, if any, personal items. Sterling took in the simple surroundings, trying to get his head around this lifestyle.

"It's so tiny," he remarked honestly with no touch of meanness. Then added, "Like where do you keep your stuff? My foyer is bigger than your whole house. Is it strange to share a bathroom? I have my own. It's connected to my room. Our house has seven bathrooms and there are only three of us, four including Nanny, plus the other help who cleans and does all the other jobs. Who cleans up for you?"

"Well, everyone takes care of their own things, and sometimes other people's too. I don't know. I don't really have any stuff. I've never thought about it."

And she honestly hadn't. To Eden, her way of life, this simple way, made sense. She'd never known anything different.

"Let's see if we can find the Sage. You should meet him." Then they heard his voice.

I'm here.

And he was. He seemed to appear before their eyes.

Follow me.

The Sage led the children to his own burre. It was set apart from the others.

Come in.

He gestured for them to enter.

Sit.

Eden and Sterling chose a bench by the central fire pit and sat close together. Sterling, who was not one to be intimidated, felt apprehensive. He knew from Eden, the Sage was the authority Inside and even though she'd described him as kind, Sterling had yet to meet an authority figure he liked.

I have something for you, the Sage told Sterling and he held out his hand. In it was a carved wooden ring. He dropped it into Sterling's palm and it felt warm there. Sterling put it on his pinky finger and it fit perfectly.

"Thank you," Sterling said solemnly, "It's just like Eden's."

Yes. We all have them here, everyone Inside, and since I think we'll be seeing more of you, I thought you should have one.

Sterling was always given anything and everything his heart desired, but for the first time he was appreciative and it felt foreign, but good.

7

Friendship

Since Eden and Sterling had behaved well together when Sterling was brought in, Mitch deemed the meetings beneficial to both children.

During the following years, the visits were regular and Sterling gradually became the brother and true best friend Eden had never had. Though Mitch was hoping it would quell Eden's curiosity about the Outside and her desire to live there, it was not to be. If anything, it made her conviction stronger.

Mitch knew Eden longed to find her family, specifically her mother. She brought up the subject in various ways and he had thus far successfully avoided it. This was her strongest motivator to go out, aside from wanting to experience Sterling's world. Besides Mitch, only the Sage knew the truth about Eden and how she'd come Inside. Mitch now questioned the judgment call he'd made years ago in the interest of his daughter's protection and in the privacy of his mind he wondered, "Is there anyone left that can teach me about her? Who was Eden's mother?" When Mitch consulted the Sage, no answers were forthcoming.

I'm afraid I can't see Eden's past. I can't give you the answers you seek.

Mitch had banked on the fact that in the Outside world people cared little about their family trees. He believed this would help to keep Eden's identity safe. He didn't want anyone to look for her. Years ago it was a curiosity to research and find out where you came from, who your kin were, and to find and contact lost relatives. Everyone knew everyone else and wanted to be connected, until eventually it shifted the other way.

Now people knew and had contact with only those they benefited from and when neither needed the other, both moved on. Being blood related was not important these days. No hard feelings. No strings attached. Some would argue relationships were more honest and followed the philosophy, "Take what you need, give what you can, then leave without looking back."

Even in his capacity as a counselor, Mitch rarely connected on a deep level with his charges, the children he worked with every day and some, for years. The end goal was to help them fit in, help them succeed as students and help them stop functioning outside of normal and acceptable. Once achieved, he often never saw them again. It was strange to be so invested in someone and then lose contact, but that was the way. Mitch considered his relationship with Sterling his biggest success. The boy had come a long way and in spite of himself, Mitch felt a genuine affection for him.

<u>8</u>

Fallen

As she grew up, Eden continued her Pure Heart Training where she and her fellow students learned empathy for the newcomers, patience and how, if ever they found themselves on the Outside, to not be tempted. All Insiders are required to take Pure Heart and everything else they choose to learn is by choice. Boys and girls, men and women gather daily in the lodge for the training. They walk from shared housing or from their individual burres. The training involves great mental and physical energy and learning and memorizing the Edicts that will keep Insiders safe and allow them to move on to the next world when their time Inside is complete.

Eden usually sat with Vita and they would send messages to each other through their minds. The instructor could sometimes tell though, then they would have to start the drill over and the whole exercise took even longer to complete. Vita was born Inside. She's one of the few. She may never go out until she's ready to pass on. Vita's parents don't love the fact that their daughter's closest friend is Eden. Eden's very presence makes them uneasy.

"Vita, aren't there other girls you could spend time with? We like Eden, but she's not the best example. She constantly interrupts and seems to enjoy stirring things up."

"I can make my own choices, besides, Eden keeps things interesting." Vita would steadfastly defend her friend, though Eden's constant questioning was a lot. One of the Edicts, "*We must not let the temporary things of the world tempt us,*" was particularly difficult for Eden to grasp. The subject of temptation was a complicated one because anyone close to Eden's age was born Inside, so they simply didn't understand the concept of temptation, except for Eden.

Children often asked the elders or their parents or teachers for examples of what might tempt them, but nothing clearly helped them understand. The only way to put it is, when you are on the Inside, all of your needs are met and because of this, you have no wants. Why would anyone want to do something they shouldn't do? Everyone knew what the Fallen went through. Redemption was rough.

When a Fallen first arrives, they are sequestered and work privately with the Sage. The children are not exposed to Fallens because it might be frightening for a child, but Eden was never frightened, only intrigued. Fallens aren't allowed in the commons until they are completely cleansed. Eden wasn't exactly sure what being cleansed involved, but she observed that the newly cleansed looked like layers were taken off them leaving nothing but the very essence of who they are. Those who modified their bodies Outside, must return to their genuine selves. It's a condition of being granted access Inside. When some return to the Outside as Ambassadors, they are hardly recognizable.

When Eden first saw Drake, he was in the commons eating at one of the long community tables, then clearing the plates, and heading out to walk the track in the fields. She'd seen him a few times and understood he was a Fallen, and she wondered what brought him here, why the Sage had allowed him in.

"I need to get a closer look at those tattoos before they fade out," Eden leaned in and whispered to Vita.

"I'm not going. You'll only get us a reprimand. We should just leave the guy alone."

Eden waited and watched for a few days, and each day the man looked healthier, the holes from the piercings filling in, the modifications turning back to his genuine self, the tattoos fading out. She was spying on him and hoping he'd sit on one of the benches. When someone sits on a bench, you are free to speak with them. It's not like no one ever talks, they do. It's just that the benches are designed for newcomers to let the community know they are ready to talk. This can take months for some, processing their former lives and shedding off all the qualities that won't work in their new selves.

The benches are not meant for children to use, but Eden was okay with not following the rules. She felt like some of the customs and rules were there just for her to push or break, to test the limits. She was working on this privately. It had been identified by more than one teacher and adult. Adults would gently tell her it wasn't preferred to think about what might happen if she did this or that. She should be grateful she didn't need to question things. She should just obey and enjoy, not be tempted. The reprimands were never harsh; they were given with love and out of concern. So what Eden learned from the newcomer on the bench that evening she found fascinating.

She just walked over and sat next to the man.

"Hi, I'm Eden. Can you tell me why you came here?"

He looked deep into her eyes and spoke very simply, as if confessing.

"I was a rich man. I owned things. I owned people. I was a bad person, but now I want to be good. Simple as that."

"What things, what people, how do you own?" Eden heard herself rapid-firing questions, hoping for answers before getting caught and reprimanded. Inside, the community shares everything, there is no ownership. Eden didn't know what the concept meant, but suspected that owning was what might lead to temptation.

"I've been here since I was a baby, but I've always wondered how a Fallen gets in. Sorry, is that rude to call you a Fallen?"

"No, not rude, it's true. I don't know if it's the same for everyone. I suspect it's not. For me, I just realized one day, I didn't like who I was, who I'd become. So, I walked out of my job and left everything. I was taking so many pills, to sleep, to stay calm, to look young. I lost touch with my essence. I went to Mental Health and checked in. An ambassador found me and brought me to the Sage. I never thought I'd find a place like this. I'm so grateful."

Drake began to tell Eden the story of his life before coming Inside, how he'd worked for Black and Silver Enterprises and he'd done things he now knew were evil and wrong, but before he got into detail, one of the elders discovered Eden on the bench and quietly reprimanded her for sitting there.

"Eden, some things are best left to the adults. You've not completed enough training to hear about the Outside yet. Please, come with me and leave this man alone."

It was true, she hadn't finished her training. Not even close, but she had been allowed Outside by her father six years ago, and it had changed her. She tried not to let on just how much. She'd seen things that were impossible to unsee and the exposure really hindered her ability to embrace the Pure Heart Training in the way she was encouraged to. The curiosity overwhelmed her.

It was equally challenging for Eden when she visited the Book Room. It was filled from floor to ceiling with books and yet, she still struggled to find what she craved. The man in charge would lead her from one to the other of the books and volumes and insist that she read at least twenty-five pages before choosing something else. This made it challenging for Eden to fulfill the reading requirement of her education and frustrating for the elders who longed to support and guide her. Eden's attention span and patience were in short supply. She only went Outside the one time, but it remained so vivid to her, it felt like yesterday. Thankfully she'd met Sterling, who was both a friend and a mine of information about life Outside.

Eventually Sterling came Inside by himself, the same as Mitch had when he was a boy and what started out as therapeutic field trips, became just regular visits until it got to the point where Sterling was in and out so often, he was a well-known presence. Sterling realized the day would come when Eden would want to go Outside again. And it did, sooner than he thought.

He arrived one day and found Eden and Vita at the pond where Eden was explaining, "I'll be leaving Inside every day. I'm finally going out again." Her friend did not understand the draw of Outside having heard so many warnings from her parents. When Eden spoke of it, Vita felt more uncomfortable than anything else.

"You're always so afraid of making a mistake Vita, you should live a little. You should come too, if your parents will let you."

Eden saw Sterling as he approached.

"Oh, good. Here comes Sterling. I know he'll be thrilled for me."

"You know I'm happy for you, I'm just worried, that's all," Vita said. But Eden was already running up to Sterling and shouting.

"Sterling, Sterling, I have the best news! I'll be coming Outside! Every day!" He looked at her quizzically.

"That's great Eden, when?"

"I'm going to go to school with you. I doubt we'll have any classes together, but we'll get to see each other all the time." Eden's enthusiasm was palpable.

"Wow, so we'll both be at U.S.A."

Vita stood up and began to walk back toward the village.

"Um, I'll see you guys later. It sounds like you have a lot to talk about."

"Vita, don't go."

"It's okay, I'll see you two later. And Eden, I'm happy for you. I know you wanted this."

"Thanks Vita," Eden called.

"So, tell me all about it. How is it going to work?" Sterling asked.

"Okay, so Dad's taking me with him every morning. We'll ride the train together and he'll drop me off, then go to his job. He'll come and get me after class or I'll meet him at Lower School. He's pretty nervous. I don't think he wants me to go to school Outside, but he promised. He's making a super big deal about me not talking about where I'm from. I'm supposed to be 'vague' if anyone asks."

"Don't worry, I seriously doubt anyone will ask you." Sterling smirked. "You'll see. People don't talk much and they're completely wrapped up in their own little worlds."

"Oh my gosh. That's exactly what my dad said. People are not too talkative."

"When will you start?"

"Next week."

Sterling tried to feign enthusiasm, but he wasn't comfortable with the idea of sharing Eden with the Outside world. He made a silent vow to be a good guide for her and to control his temper. He knew she was safe if she stayed Inside and he felt it his responsibility to keep her equally safe in his world.

9

Upper School for Adolescents

Eden shucked off the shorts and tunic and stood in her underwear looking through the racks of clothes in Clothing. The goal was not to stand out, it was to blend in. For the second time in her life, that she could remember, she was going Outside and would be, for five days a week to attend Upper School for Adolescents. It was Sterling's last year at U.S.A. and his behavior had improved due to the fact that he was a well-established loner among his peers. He stayed away from people and avoided conversation. Fairly easy to accomplish in Upper School, as most kids rarely spoke out loud preferring to send messages over their devices even when standing close enough to touch each other. Sterling was blissfully unaware of female interest in him. Occasionally he would need something from someone and it seemed all he had to do was ask, and other students, girls in particular, were willing to abide. He relished the power of persuasion, but rarely chose to use it. When invited to events or parties, he declined consistently mumbling, "No thanks. I'm busy." until the invites were few and far between.

No one remembered how troubled he'd been years before, including the ones who'd been victims of his uncontrollable fury, an advantage of the collective short attention span. Since meeting Eden, it wasn't that Sterling was no longer ever angry. He was. He was just better able to control it so it didn't affect his life the way it had before. And if he wasn't with her, just the thought of Eden, calmed him in a way nothing else could.

The first time Eden sat in class, it didn't seem like much time had passed. She'd never been expected to sit for so long, or be silent for so long, but this new method of learning piqued her interest just enough. Mitch was concerned Eden would stand out and draw attention. He wondered how she would grasp all the technology. She'd been allowed to grow up without it. There was one television Inside, which no one used. There was an old, outdated computer too, which sat idle. When the Fallen came in, they were glad to leave a world filled with technology behind for a simple life. Most were shocked at how little they missed it. Mitch stayed current on technology out of necessity, using it only as a tool to do his job, but he too, preferred the simple life of Inside. He needn't have worried about his daughter. Eden had no trouble at all; she observed and followed the other students' lead. A few girls stared, distracted by her presence and Eden found she enjoyed it.

The new knowledge entered and settled like dust motes in the minds of the students where over time the layers would build up, and with little effort, new mental skills were acquired. Students sat in straight-backed chairs with headsets on while instructors programmed each one's individual input and monitored their progress. After the morning session, Eden found Sterling waiting for her. Walking to lunch with him she said, "I've never sat so still for so long; I can see why it makes you nuts. On the upside, it's pretty easy to learn stuff, I hardly have to focus."

At the lunch hour, in the cafeteria, Eden tried her best to seem nonchalant as she followed Sterling's lead, carrying her tray through the line. The dazzling array of foods, smells, and colors overwhelmed her just as they had the last time she was Outside. Nothing looked familiar, but it all looked tempting and smelled exquisite. Eden wanted badly to pile a bit of everything on the plate, but noticed what the other students took and thought better of it.

"Are there any donuts?" Eden had a fond memory of the treat she'd had the last time she was out with Mitch. The serving lady gave her a look of annoyance which conveyed quite clearly the message, "Why are you addressing me?" Then she touched Eden's hand holding the tray and said in a nicer, but still impatient tone, "Move along, please. Don't back up the line." Eden didn't reply, but paused before continuing. Later that evening, the lunch lady panicked as angry red boils appeared out of nowhere from her fingertips to her shoulders.

"Don't ask." Sterling said as he playfully pushed Eden along.

"The lunch ladies aren't big on requests. I'll find you a donut later, weirdo."

Having her here, really here finally, made him smile and want to pinch himself. The only way to explain it was that with Eden, he felt real and when he wasn't with her, he counted the hours until he could be again. Though he wanted her to know his world so she could better know him, he felt more at ease in her world, Inside, where people were content and life was simple.

"Hey, ask your dad if you can come over tomorrow. I want to show you my house." Sterling had been describing his life and home-life to Eden for years, and she had built it up in her imagination and dreams and was eager to see if reality matched her pictures.

"Maybe I'll ask him for next week. Get settled in a bit. He's still not too keen on me coming out every day. But, don't worry, I know he trusts you."

10

Silver Estate

Eden and Mitch settled into a routine. They exited together each morning and returned late afternoon in time for dinner. The feedback from Mitch's colleagues was positive to his face, but each secretly wondered about his daughter and how she was raised and why they'd never seen her before. They knew Mitch was a private person, choosing not to share much of his personal life. He came to his job, worked with the children, completed paperwork, attended meetings as necessary, and left. His private life was private. No one knew if he was married or in a relationship or what part of town he lived in, and until now, no one cared. Not in a mean way, just everyone was in their own world. Eden changed that. Questions and comments percolated.

"I never knew he had a kid."

"He looks awfully young to have a teenager."

"Is he with the mother, do you think?"

Once Eden was Outside, she was noticed. Something about her demanded noticing. She was no good at being quiet or blending. The effect she had, though not negative, was nonetheless unsettling. Students were drawn to her immediately and they began talking even when they weren't in Conversation class, even when it was not required. They were curious to find out more.

"It's going well, I'd say." Eden pushed up next to Sterling as more people piled into the compartment. With little room to move, Eden noticed the care people took to avoid touching. Each person had their invisible bubble. The train was packed this time of afternoon, the air heavy with scents of relief and exhaustion. These were the workers heading home to shared housing or to their families. It wasn't often Sterling took this public form of travel. He had his own car, but Eden wanted to see and try all things, so here they were, riding with the masses. She could make the most mundane activity seem exciting and fun.

A red-scarfed lady stole glances at the two teenagers, remembering a time when she, too, felt happiness, and realizing she hadn't felt it in quite some time.

"We'll get off a little way from where I live. We'll have a short walk, and then we'll punch in at the gates." Sterling was half talking to himself.

"Push the button Eden, we're getting off here." He handed her a small plastic piece. "Oh, and insert this nose guard."

The train stopped and they jumped off quickly. They were on the outskirts of the main city. It seemed quieter. It was an area best described as one that people passed through while on their way to somewhere else. The scenery wasn't much to look at. The roads were kept paved, but that was it.

"I hope no one sees us walking." Sterling was concerned and didn't want to answer questions. The only people ever seen walking this road were house servants, and Eden and Sterling hardly looked the part.

"I probably should've just driven us. I don't like being noticed." But then it occurred to Sterling that even if he was seen it was highly unlikely anyone would recognize him, or care. He was just being paranoid.

Up ahead the large gates of the compound loomed, looking preposterously out of place and this struck Sterling as funny when considering it through Eden's perspective. The giant wrought iron sign read, "Black and Silver Estates." All this space, while others lived crammed into small apartments. His own house was so big it was easy to get lost or be forgotten.

"Wait, why is your last name on that giant sign? Does your father own this place?" Eden asked Sterling.

"Yes, at least half of it, and it positively kills him that his partner's name comes before his," Sterling said while rolling his eyes.

"I'd like to meet your dad."

"No. You wouldn't. Trust me."

They were admitted without incident, the gateman bored and unaffected.

"No need for protection in here. It's filtered." Sterling popped out the nose guard and shoved it in his pocket. Eden did the same.

Pausing to take it in, at first she had no words.

"It's like everything's arranged, planned." Indeed, it was. There were flowers in patterns and circles, the colors symmetrical and beautiful, but not at all natural like the chaotic wildflowers Eden was used to. The landscaping threw her off. She'd not seen plants arranged before and trimmed to look tamed. Yes, tamed was the word that best suited the place, tamed or controlled.

They walked up and stood in front of side-by-side enormous black wooden doors and waited as Sterling punched in a code on a side panel. He led the way into the large foyer, where the ceiling soared over 20 feet high. Afternoon light streamed into windows made of little pieces of colored glass forming pictures. "Stained glass," Sterling pointed, "brought in from who knows where."

The floors were a shiny, bright white marble. Ahead was a large open space with spiral staircases to the left and right. Further on, Eden could see passages leading off on both sides.

"This feels like a sacred place, like we shouldn't be here," she breathed in a whisper.

"I told you it was different, so overdone and ostentatious! Do you hate it? We can leave."

"I don't hate it. I can't believe it." And she truly couldn't. Sure, there were palaces described in the books she read, but to be in one herself was unbelievable.

"You haven't seen anything yet. If you're this excited about the entry, prepare to really be blown away. Let's go get a snack, I know how much you love to snack!"

It was true. Eden loved the whole "snacking" idea. Inside, food was never eaten except at designated times where everyone sat together and shared a meal. You didn't just grab food whenever you wanted. There was also little variety. Everything was healthy and made fresh. It tasted good, but Eden never craved it.

Sterling summoned the house cook on a keypad in the kitchen, and a lady in a crisp uniform showed up minutes later.

"What can I make you, Master Sterling?"

"Whatever. Maybe something colorful and sweet, my friend likes sweets."

Eden looked at him and felt a rush of pride. She liked being called his friend.

"Right away." The cook responded, then set to work making a tray with fruit, crackers and cheeses and a variety of fancy cookies, all the while wondering who the girl was. It was rare to have guests at the Silver mansion. Even Sterling's parents seldom had friends over and the cook spent many hours doing nothing but waiting until she was asked to prepare something.

Sterling showed Eden the library, the study, his room, and they took a quick peek into his father's office. Then they circled back to the kitchen, pausing on the tour.

"Grab something and I'll show you some more."

Eden took a handful of cookies, leaving the fruit behind. Next, Sterling led her to a large open atrium with a glass covered ceiling where there was a large pool.

"Is this seriously a pool? In your house? Can we jump in?" Eden was thrilled with the idea and didn't consider for a second the fact that she had no swimsuit or extra clothes. Sterling laughed and gently pulled her back from the water's edge before she could impulsively dive in.

"Another time. I promise. Your dad won't trust me if I send you home soaked." For about a second, he marveled at the fact that he was being the mature one, taking responsibility and not being impulsive himself.

Across the room, a figure lay in a lounge chair. She wore a pink filmy dress and large sunglasses.

"Sterling, darling, is that you?" The scratchy voice asked.

"Who is with you? Is that a girl?"

Sterling was counting on neither of his parents being around. He never brought friends home and rarely spoke to his parents. Of late, conversations with his father centered on how Sterling planned to spend his adulthood because he, "sure as hell wasn't going to laze around the house and not contribute." Sterling wasn't sure what he could contribute exactly, but there was constant talk of the Silver Empire and how they would work together to expand it. Eden walked over and sat on the edge of the lounge.

"Hi Mrs. Silver, my name's Eden. I'm Sterling's friend, more of a partner in crime really." Eden laughed as she held out her hand for Sterling's mom. Eden certainly knew how to charm. The woman paused and then grasped Eden's warm hand in her cold, boney one.

"You're beautiful," she said, struck by Eden's eyes which were the perfect shade of violet just then.

Mr. Silver seemed to be there all at once. His presence and cologne seemed to fill the room.

"Why haven't we met you before? 'Eden,' did you say it was?"

"Yes, her name is Eden, and no you haven't met her, you haven't met any of my friends." The words were more forceful than Sterling intended as he tried to steer Eden away from his parents, but it was clear his father would not have it.

"I wasn't aware you had friends. I thought you prided yourself on being a loner," his father baited.

"Oh, well, I wasn't allowed on the Outside before, but now I am," Eden explained.

"The Outside? I'm not sure what you mean." The large man touched his beard and seemed to want a reply. Sterling tried desperately to signal Eden. He wanted nothing more than for her to shut up just then. Why could she not just shut up?

"Oh, it's complicated. I actually live……," but Sterling cut her off mid-sentence.

"Wow, look at the time. I have to get Eden home."

Without waiting for a response, Sterling quickly led Eden away.

"Nice to finally meet you," she shouted over her shoulder as they left the atrium.

When the two were out of earshot, Sterling said, "Eden, you have to be careful what you say around my parents, especially my father. They're super shallow and judgmental. Oh, and nosy, so nosy, as you probably noticed. I don't like to share my personal life with them, and I don't want them knowing about Inside. Okay?"

Eden giggled, "Sure, whatever you say."

11

Truth

Meeting Sterling's mother made Eden wonder even more about her own. First she went to the Sage, but he did not give her the information she wanted.

Eden, dear, it's not my story to tell. You need to speak with your father. Don't be afraid to ask.

Mitch knew it was a conversation he couldn't put off with Eden and worried and wondered, *How can I satisfy her curiosity about her mother, her family, when I have no information to give? I lied by omission.* He struggled for the words to explain to his daughter her origins. Then Eden approached him as they sat by the fire and she explained.

"I've been trying to research my family tree and I can't find anything, Dad. I didn't tell you sooner because I didn't want to hurt you, but I need to know. What if I have relatives, maybe some half brothers or sisters? I look at the other students in class and wonder if I'm related to them. I want to see my mom. I want to know how you met, why she left me. I'm sorry Dad. Please don't be angry."

Mitch struggled for the right words.

"Eden, I'm not angry at all. Please know how much I love you. You are my daughter," and he paused, nervous and also relieved to finally unburden himself with the truth. "But I am not your biological father. I don't know if we're actually related at all."

Mitch inhaled deeply. He locked eyes with Eden. He began the story he'd rehearsed many times in his head.

"Let me try to explain. I stopped in to see my parents and it'd been a long time between visits. When I saw you with them, I was shocked. I almost didn't see you at all. If you hadn't whimpered, I might not have. I was almost nineteen at the time, almost an adult, and I was embarrassed that my parents lived like that. It was my secret shame. Each time I visited, I hoped for something different, but with my parents and the past life I'd known, it was as if time stood still. Nothing changed at all."

He paused, waiting for a reaction.

"Why was I with them Dad, did you leave me there?"

"Oh, Eden, it's so complicated. I'll go back to the beginning and maybe it will make more sense."

Mitch took another deep breath and continued.

"My parents raised me outside, like "out-of-doors" outside. We had a shelter they built and there were others. When I was very young, it was still somewhat safe being out in the air. The news and the media constantly warned that it was becoming dangerous, really unsafe and unhealthy, but no one believed it. Everyone thought the problem would be solved or would go away somehow on its own. Just fix itself, I suppose. No one was really willing to listen, pay close attention, or make changes. Then, all at once, things got extreme and the changes, the horrible warnings of things we didn't expect to see in our lifetimes, were upon us.

The government stepped in and the tubes and tunnels were built. The air was filtered. We started using the sun as energy and halted the pollution. But the damage was done. And you can't believe how quickly it happened. But it was too little effort, too late. Everyone was encouraged to stay out of the elements and spend little time if any in unfiltered air, but my parents refused. They wouldn't comply. They loved their freedom. They didn't want to be told where to live, be assigned work or be told what to do or be forced to take compliance pills or be made to give up alcohol. They chose to live in the periphery and to keep me with them. I was over five so they couldn't surrender me without consequence, not that they considered it. I was no trouble to them."

Mitch paused, letting the information sink in.

"So the people went in?" Eden seemed to be speaking more to herself than to Mitch, as if realizing something for the first time. She looked at Mitch.

"They are forgetting, Dad. They are already forgetting what nature is like for real. They just use their screens. And it's good enough."

"I know. That's why I wanted you safe Inside. I wanted you to see the world as it could be, simple, stripped down, uncomplicated, real. People come Inside to take a time out or to heal. I wanted it to just be your world, all you knew. I'm sorry."

"Don't be, Dad. I love that this is my home, that you're my father. It's nothing against you. I've just always felt there was more and that I needed to be a part of it. When I listen to the Temptation lessons, I feel like they're tailored to me. Instead of resisting, I want to do the things I shouldn't. This might seem weird, but I know that can't come from you, so it must be from my mother, whoever she is, and maybe knowing her will help me understand myself. I've never told you, but I can make things happen using my will, bad things. I've tried to control it, but I like the power too."

Her head was bowed as she whispered this truth. She found it impossible to look into her father's eyes and was grateful for the semi-darkness of their small burre. Eden had never admitted this deep secret before and wasn't ashamed, just unsure how her dad would react.

Mitch had suspected, but never confirmed it. Thoughts ran quickly through his mind. Was this the proof that Eden would not succeed the Sage? It had to be him, Mitch, but something about the prophecy just didn't add up. It was true Mitch was not restricted to one world or the other as all adults were, but only Eden had the violet eyes, a deep, deep blue, but in the sun, a distinctly purple hue. Mitch's own were a constant coffee brown, whether Inside or Outside. As far as he knew, the Sage was never wrong before. Were they misinterpreting the message? Or maybe the new Sage had yet to be revealed. The Sage felt confident they would know.

All in due time.

"Eden, you know I love you no matter what. There is nothing you could do to ever change my mind."

Mitch continued telling Eden the story of her beginnings.

"Oh Eden, I never left you there at all. I almost missed you. I was distracted, focused on seeing my parents quickly, leaving money, and going away. It was always hard for me to be there and see how they lived, how I lived before I left. As I was leaving, I heard a sound, a little sound like a baby, but it couldn't be a baby. Were they keeping a puppy?

I asked what made the sound; then I walked over to where it was coming from. It was you, Eden. You were in a little basket in the corner and I swear you were trying to talk to me."

"What did I say?" Eden wanted to know.

"You reached for me and smiled and I imagined you said, 'Take me,' and I knew I wasn't leaving without you. I told my parents I would take you. They agreed it was best."

What they didn't say was, the baby made others uncomfortable and some of their friends had mentioned black magic. Mitch kept this to himself.

"I couldn't live with you at my apartment. It wasn't practical. I shared it with three others and promised to look for another place as soon as I brought you home. Then, just weeks later, my mother died, and it occurred to me that

74

I should go Inside. It would be the safest place. The Sage would help me and so would the women. They would know what to do with a baby. There was one glitch. I was nineteen which meant I'd have to choose to stay Inside with you, leave you and not get back in, or not take you in at all. The choice was easy. It was only later I discovered I could move between the worlds. And that is another story for another day."

"So Dad, who am I?" She paused, and asked, "Are we brother and sister?"

This was what Mitch dreaded. He could not answer the question. It had haunted him for the past fifteen years and he saw no clear way to figure it out.

"Eden, I don't know for sure. I didn't see my parents often so it's possible my mom could have hidden a pregnancy. She was only 39 when she died. I went back to my dad to get some questions answered after my mom died, but it was useless. He told me nothing, and he died a short while later."

"Doesn't the Sage know? I thought he knew everything."

"He doesn't know who you are either, Eden."

As Mitch said the words, he felt it came out wrong and tried to put it gently.

"What I mean is, he can't read you, Eden. The Sage can only see your present, not your past. There are things we can do Outside though, if you decide you really need to know. We can investigate, do DNA tests. I just want you to understand, you may not like what we find."

Mitch decided not to elaborate further on this point.

The fire was burning down. It was late.

"Let's sleep on it. We don't need to make any decisions tonight."

<u>12</u>

Designed

Fifteen years earlier, the sudden surge of pollution had caused untold damage to people's health. Greyson and Celia Black, like so many other couples, were not able to have a child. Celia Black had heard about the technology, but didn't want the stigma. Wouldn't everyone know, or at least suspect their child was artificially created? It was a concern even though Celia felt sure most of their friends and acquaintances used the technology, though no one admitted it. It was all in secret, but you could tell the kids were designer babies, many coincidentally having the popular traits of the time they were born.

One year it was all blondes with green eyes, the next, dark hair with dark eyes. If a family could afford it, they may even have two. It was always a boy first, then a second boy or sometimes a girl, if the wife fancied it, but never a girl first. What Celia Black didn't know, (no one did till it happened to them), was with the technology came steep risks. It was still relatively new. The babies didn't always turn out "right."

So when Celia was at her most desperate, she went to Rose Silver's house to seek advice from the closest thing she had to a friend. Celia was certain Sterling was a designer baby.

"Oh, no dear, I'm so sorry you're having trouble." Rose paused, her mouth forming a thin, tense line.

"That must be just awful for you, just awful. But, no, Sterling is our own child, no lab work involved. That's why you didn't see me for nine months. That little guy had me sick during my whole pregnancy, couldn't even leave the house, could I?" She sighed as if remembering.

Both women were part of this charade and neither would speak honestly.

"Yes, yes, now I remember how very sick you were."

Her hope of finding an honest sympathetic friend was fading fast, as she realized Rose Silver was not going to admit that she, too, could not conceive a child and that Sterling was designed.

Celia decided to take a different approach.

"Ok then, do you know who I could contact?"

She laid it out for Rose, still hoping the woman would help her.

"I want a child. I can't have one. I am not going to Abandoned Children to choose one, as I'm sure you agree would be a bad idea. This leaves me with only one possibility as I see it. So do you know anyone who could help me?"

Rose pretended to think hard for a moment, then she answered.

"I think I can get you a name." She added, "And you didn't get it from me."

"Of course, of course, and thank you so much."

And they left it at that, each woman glad to end the awkward conversation.

Two weeks later, Celia and Greyson Black, under the cover of darkness, consulted with the scientist who would create a child for them. They provided the DNA samples and were shocked at the limitless choices for adult height, weight, amount of body hair, skin tone, facial structure, and even something called "personality traits". After some discussion they agreed on a male child, as virtually every couple did. He would have golden hair and green eyes, like Celia's. He would reach a height of six feet at adulthood, a whole four inches taller than his father. Celia wished to have a child who favored her genes over her husband's, as her husband, in his natural state, was not very attractive. Mr. Black had undergone extensive plastic surgery and it had helped to make him more appealing. Celia considered herself a great beauty, but she too had had her share of modifications.

The parents were given a three dimensional image of the projected baby and were even able to watch him grow up in a sped-up video so real it was almost unbelievable. The created child was guaranteed to have 80% to 85% of his parents' genes so he would be a strong DNA match and no one need ever know he wasn't conceived and born in the usual way. This also assuaged the egos of the parents who while wanting their child genetically linked to themselves, also wanted a child who was somehow even better. Oddly, no one ever asked about the other 15 to 20%.

<u>13</u>

Family

After the last close call, Sterling hadn't brought Eden home again. They managed to get the same Conversation time and lunch hour, so for now, it was just nice to see each other every day. At home it seemed his parents were taking a sudden unsolicited interest in him. For the past two weeks they joined him at dinner, where the three sat at the long table meant for twelve, staring at their plates and stumbling through stilted conversation. Mr. and Mrs. Silver tried to bring up Eden, but Sterling did his best to steer the conversation away from her, feigning interest in his father's business. This was usually a fail-safe topic as Mr. Silver loved nothing more than to talk about the Silver Empire, always conveniently leaving off his partner's name, "Black" from the title. Finally, Sterling's parents insisted he invite Eden back, promising not to be intrusive. Sterling attempted to explain.

"Look, Eden's had a different childhood. She doesn't come from rich parents. It's just Eden and her father, she doesn't even have a mom and she's sensitive about it."

Unfortunately, this explanation did not quell his parents' interest.

His father spoke, trying his best to keep his voice even.

"Look Son, we've allowed you to do as you pleased and we've never been involved in your friendships, or lack of friendships, but it's time you consider who you hang around with. I don't think that a motherless girl who is not in our social class is a good choice. How is she able to attend your school?"

Sterling's mom tried to smooth his father's rough edges and put it more delicately.

"Well, at least we know she must be gifted, or she wouldn't be admitted to Upper School."

To which Sterling replied, "No one said we were getting married. She's 15 and we are friends. That's it. You wonder why I don't share my life with you? It's because the second I do, you have nothing but criticism." Sterling left the table and retreated to his room with a feeling of dread. He thought about how he could best instruct Eden to behave around his parents to avoid their nosiness.

14

Questions

Eden went out with Mitch for the first two days of the week, but had to stay in for the last three and it wasn't likely she'd get out for the weekend. Thus, there was no way for her to communicate with Sterling. She knew he would wonder and worry about her, but the deal was, if Mitch did not go Outside, she didn't either. Her father told her he had business to attend to Inside and she'd have to miss school. Eden didn't fight it; she knew she must be grateful. It was giving her time to catch up with Vita, whom she realized she'd neglected since going Outside regularly. She also realized in Vita she had a true friend, unlike the girls Outside who struck her as disingenuous.

Eden was trying hard to convince Vita she should come Outside with her. She had it all planned. They could finish Upper School and Specialize. They could get jobs and get an apartment with the other commoners. They wouldn't be rich, but they wouldn't be poor. And they could eat as much glorious food as they wanted. Eden once tried to smuggle a treat in for Vita, but it had disappeared as soon as she'd entered. The boundaries separating Outside from Inside were strict, no exceptions.

"I don't want to be rich or poor or a Commoner or anything else Outside. In here we have everything we need. You are way too obsessed about food, Eden. I don't think that's a good thing, and what about the air? You told me yourself, it's not even safe to breathe. No, I don't want it. I'm just hoping you'll be able to go back and forth after you're an adult. I'd miss you terribly if you left me forever."

The more Vita learned about Eden's experience Outside, the less she wanted to go.

"I've heard some things lately, Eden. I wasn't trying to eavesdrop, but once I heard, I couldn't leave."

"Vita, I'm proud of you. It sounds like me forcing you to play Spy and Report is going to pay off. What did you learn?"

"Let me start by saying, it was purely by accident I overheard Mitch and the Sage. I was just walking and I heard them and I stopped to listen. I know the conversation was private, but I think I should tell you."

Clearly Vita was not comfortable being deceptive.

"It doesn't matter Vita, no sense feeling guilty. Now tell me what you know."

"It's not good, Eden. It's Mitch. He's sick, and from what I could tell the Sage thinks it's from going in and out so much and not using any protective measures or taking any pills. It's been really hard on his body."

"What does it mean?" Eden had never thought of life without her dad.

"He can't really be sick. I mean doesn't everyone think he'll take over for the Sage? Including the Sage?"

"I know the elders used to think that, but not anymore. Everyone's been talking about it, Eden. You just haven't been paying attention. I heard your dad say, 'I don't have long' and also, 'It's not me, I'm not the next Sage. I'm only a messenger, but I don't know the message'. It's not him, Eden. He's not the next Sage."

"Then who?" Eden was confused and feeling guilty. She'd been so busy with her own concerns. How had she missed this?

"Vita, did you hear anything else?"

"I heard the Sage say, 'I don't know the message either. I was so certain it was you, maybe I missed the signs. I could dissolve the field now and the worlds would merge,' at least I think that's what he said. I couldn't hear much else, but it sounded like your dad wants to wait. I don't think either of them want the worlds to merge, we'd lose all our protection then."

"What do you think it means for us?" Eden asked.

"I don't know. I'm sorry I said anything. I had no business, but I hope I misunderstood."

"Don't be sorry Vita, and thanks. I'm glad you told me."

Eden embraced her friend for a good long while. Her thoughts seemed to be running faster than she could grasp them. She needed to think. She walked to the meadow and found her favorite bench empty. She sat down and tried to slow her mind. She wanted to examine just one thought at a time. If her father was dying, what would become of her, of all of Inside? It was a widely accepted belief that Mitch was to be the next Sage. If not him, then who? Eden dared not think about the other part of the prophecy, but now it made sense when her dad had mentioned a threat to the Inside. He'd also said the key was through the children. She racked her brain to remember the lessons from Pure Heart and the times she heard the Sage speak directly to the people Inside.

Every once in a while the Sage would speak at Pure Heart Training, but usually the Elders delivered the lesson and guided the meditations of the day. There were certain edicts and stories everyone Inside knew, like the role of the Sage.

I was chosen as Sage many years ago and here I have remained. I can be of help to you. I can offer guidance, but I cannot intervene. I cannot change people. Most importantly, I cannot alter fate. You control your own destiny.

Everyone knew this, but no one, including the Sage knew how long he would stay and what would become of Inside when he was called on. If life was proceeding well, no one wanted to think about it.

There is one who will succeed me. I will pass the prophecies onto him and he will begin to communicate the prophecy himself. He or she will be a bright angel, one to help, never hurt. The Sage will be born a human under poor circumstances. When the full prophecy is revealed, we will know the next Sage and we will accept them.

There is also a dark force coming in the form of a human. We must be aware. We know not when or how, but we will be tempted, and this dark force can destroy Inside if we allow it.

Eden suspected there was more to the prophecy, but this was all the Sage chose to share with the people. It dawned on her now why the lessons involving temptation were so important. They must be part of the training and preparation to fight this dark force. She hoped tomorrow she could go Outside again. It was easier out there. Her dad was so important to her, but she knew in her heart if she lost him, she would leave Inside forever. Outside was more true to who she was. It was so difficult to be good all the time.

15

Mean Girls

Sterling was bouncing up and down on his toes, swinging his arms and looking like he was preparing to run a race. His dark bangs flopped over one eye making him look disheveled, but in a handsome sort of way. He had not made it Inside the past weekend and Eden was absent for three days last week. He tried to glimpse her this morning, but either she was absent again or he just missed her. Now he waited, hoping she would show up for Conversation, the only class they had together.

In she strode, with a group of girls, her golden hair perfectly reflecting the light. Engrossed in conversation, she almost passed right by him.

"Oh, Sterling, join us. These girls were just going to show me how to do my hair." Eden flipped her hair in his direction and laughed. Sterling joined them, but something felt off. His brain blanked for a minute and was taken over with an image of the thin red haired girl, Ember. She was yanking Eden's hair with all her might as a second girl grabbed scissors and chopped off a huge hunk leaving what looked like an uneven scar on the back of Eden's head where her beautiful golden hair should be. He snapped out of it, the image disappearing as quickly as it came. He composed himself, relieved to see Eden's hair, beautiful as always, and he joined the girls at the table to practice small talk.

"So Eden, I feel like I should point out that you're getting fat." This blunt comment came from Ember, the red headed girl.

Sterling interjected, "Ember, I think you FAIL at small talk. That's an insult, and no way to speak to Eden. You must have slept through Manners Class." If hitting a girl wouldn't get him thrown out of school and possibly into jail, he might've done it right then. He wanted nothing more than to punch her right in her smug, upturned nose.

But Eden only laughed. "Fat? You think I'm fat? Is it because of this?" She grabbed the skin around her abdomen where she was developing a small belly.

"Who cares?! I love food!"

The three other girls exchanged unsure glances. They were confused. This was not the reaction they had expected.

"Why don't you just take pills? There's one to take your hunger away."

"Or"..., said another girl, "take the one that helps you burn the calories. Either way, you don't need to get fat. No one gets fat anymore."

"If they can afford not to, that is," piped in a third girl.

Eden replied, "Um, thanks for your concern, but I don't care, I really don't, and I'm certainly not taking any pills. You people Outside take so many, they're turning your brains to mush. None of you can even think for yourselves. Honestly, it's pathetic."

Ember looked paler than usual and maybe frightened, too. She wondered what Eden meant by, "Outside."

"What a strange girl," she thought, but what she said was, "Sorry Eden. I was only trying to be helpful. You shouldn't be embarrassed if you can't afford treatments."

"It's a shame there's no treatment for your horrible acne." Eden shot back as she stood to leave. She paused, leaned in close to Ember and reached over to stroke Ember's perfect ivory cheek. All the girls couldn't hide their disappointment when Sterling stood and followed Eden. Then they whispered among themselves.

"I have no idea what he sees in her."

"Can you imagine?"

"He finally decides to be social and that's who he picks?"

"She's obviously not from money. Look at her clothes."

"What a waste!"

Ember checked her reflection in the bathroom mirror before heading to her next class. What was that? A pimple? It seemed to grow larger as she looked at it. Then a second one popped up on her chin, then two more. *Oh my gosh. Eden was right,* she thought, but she'd never had a pimple in her life. There was a pill to make sure of it. She cringed in dismay and headed to the nurse's office with her head down, hoping her long red hair would hide her face. All she wanted to do was get home without being seen.

By the time her driver arrived, half of her face was purple and swollen with angry, red pustules. Logically, she knew it was impossible, yet her gut told her this was purely Eden's fault. She wasn't so much angry as fearful of what else Eden might be capable of.

16

Avarice

Mr. Silver sat in his gleaming mahogany office leaning over his desk with his head in his hands. He was thoroughly exasperated, just waiting for the pill he'd popped to take away the acid in his stomach, and the other one to relieve his pounding headache. Once again he turned what should have been a pleasant evening into a fighting match with his son. Sterling had invited the girl, Eden, home after school at his insistence. Mr. Silver thought her odd, and something he could not quite name made him feel ill-at-ease around her, though she acted normal enough. Eager to learn more about her, he'd suggested she call her father and ask if she might stay for dinner. The girl said she had no way to call; she just needed to get back by dusk, but thanked him for the offer.

That got him wondering. *Were there still people in this world, other than the homeless, too poor to have a phone? Why did his son feel the need to befriend this girl? Why was he trying to keep his parents from getting to know her?*

Mr. Silver could not shake the feeling his son was hiding something from him. There was something unnerving about the girl and try as he might, he could not figure out what it was. So when Sterling returned after taking her home, Mr. Silver pressed his son for more details. The more he asked, the less his son was willing to share until finally Rose Silver stepped in and offered her two cents.

"Oh, Avi, what does it matter? She seems like a sweet girl to me, and she's so beautiful. I've never seen eyes like that. It's like they're violet, just gorgeous. Besides, she and Sterling are only friends. We want him to have friends, remember? Let's just leave him alone right now. Sterling honey, you can go to your room. You're excused."

Sterling was all too happy to get out of there. He knew eventually his father would not back down with the questions and if he found out about the Inside and how a place like that still existed, a place unspoiled by humans, Mr. Silver would make it his mission to acquire it. Sometimes Sterling's father disgusted him with his greed. No matter what he had, or how much, it was never enough to satisfy him.

After dinner, an escape was what Mr. Silver felt he needed to clear his mind and relax. He went to his library and sunk into his favorite leather recliner. He put in his earphones and strapped the sensory glasses on. He programmed a peaceful setting and within minutes was transported to a beautiful unspoiled place. He felt the breeze and could almost taste the freshness of the air. His virtual-self walked the meadow path, and he settled on a hammock strung between two shady trees to take a nap.

When the program was finished, he still wasn't quite as calm as he would like, but instead of immersing himself again in another program, he decided to leave his library, walk through the house, and go to sleep in his real bed, in his real world.

As he reached to pull the chain on his nightstand lamp, something caught his eye from across the room. It was his wife's purple robe flung on the back of a chair. It was more of a violet, actually. Something about that color clicked in his mind, and it sent a chill through his whole body.

<u>17</u>

Funeral

Saturday morning Sterling was dragged, against his will, to the funeral service for Greyson Black, of Black and Silver Enterprises. Until that very morning, he hadn't even known the man had died. The Blacks were Sterling's godparents, so chosen by his parents, but he wasn't close to them. They lived in the same compound as the Silvers, but Sterling rarely saw them, and couldn't even recall the last time he'd seen Mrs. Black. After the service, he hugged Celia Black and mumbled, "I'm sorry for your loss. He was a wonderful man." Then his father subtly pushed him aside and spoke to Mrs. Black in a low voice. He dispensed with condolences and got straight to the point.

"Celia, look, I just need you to sign these papers. It'll only take a minute."

Mr. Silver opened his briefcase and was ready with a pen in hand.

"Avi, you know I'm not signing anything without consulting my lawyer first, and there's a private matter I need to look into. It's not that I don't trust you. This has all just been so....sudden, so unexpected."

With that the black-clad lady broke down into tears, the sobs racking her slim shoulders, her made-up face turning clownish and scary.

"Here, use this." Mr. Silver handed her the handkerchief from his suit pocket. Celia took it, dabbed at her tears and wiped her runny nose.

To all who knew them, she and her late husband appeared to have a happy life, despite the frequent comments and whispers among their friends about how sad, as well as unlucky, it was that they were never able to have a child after their first one died. What a shame, with all that money.

"Sure Celia, I didn't mean to upset you. I can have my lawyer answer any questions, we can talk next week. This is so hard. You know how much I loved Grey. He was like a brother to me."

Mr. Silver gave her a quick hug then and said, "I'll call you soon."

Celia handed back the soiled handkerchief, and Mr. Silver shoved it in his pocket.

Sterling's parents had felt it appropriate and insisted he attend the service since the Blacks were his godparents. Mr. Black and his father were business partners and old school friends. Each man came from wealthy families and each was the only surviving child of his parents. All the other siblings, six between them, had passed away, and all within the last ten years, leaving only Avarice Silver and Greyson Black as the main two shareholders of the Black and Silver Empire, or as Sterling secretly thought of it, the "B.S. Empire."

In the car after the memorial service, Sterling stared at the back of his parents' heads which seemed to radiate smugness, his mom with her perfectly styled and shaped hairdo and his father, his black hair shot with a bit of silver, and he could not resist the urge to comment.

"Dad, was it really necessary to approach Mrs. Black about business stuff the day of her husband's funeral?"

"Son, you know nothing about business. Celia can be sure I'll take care of her. I'm only asking her to put me in charge, officially. It's business."

"That would increase your wealth by how much? Does it even matter? I mean really, how much does one person need?"

Mr. Silver's face turned red and his knuckles white as he gripped the steering wheel and struggled to control his temper. This was not the first time lately his son had said something utterly absurd. *For goodness sakes, this kid stood to inherit a fortune and acted as if he didn't care, the spoiled brat. His consolation was, he, Avarice Silver, was not planning to go anywhere for a long time, a very long time if the pills worked as promised, and hopefully long enough to mold his son into a proper heir and businessman so his legacy might continue.*

"Mom, how old was Uncle Greyson, anyway? It seems odd that he died so suddenly. Weren't you guys with them just last week?"

Mrs. Silver removed her earphones.

"What dear, did you say something?"

Sterling had a moment of clarity then, realizing just how frustrating it was to grow up with these two. No wonder he had anger issues. He put on a stiff smile and repeated the question.

"He was 56, I believe. I think it was brain shock. Celia said he felt 'off' and went to bed early. Then he died in his sleep. There's nothing she could have done."

"Hmm, it seems like what she could have done was take him to a doctor if he wasn't well," Sterling countered.

"And wasn't he taking those same expensive pills you take, Dad?"

"Sterling! Stop being a brat. Now you're giving me a headache, and I don't like the tone of this conversation."

Mrs. Silver fumbled around in her purse.

"Damn. I left my pills at home. Avi, drive faster, before this headache gets any worse."

Not one week later, Mr. Silver was feeling smug and thankful. He sat with the signed papers in his hands, and the results were even better than he dared hope for. After consulting with her lawyer, Celia Black decided the best course of action was to let Avi buy her out. What did it matter that the Black family name would no longer be part of Black and Silver Enterprises? It wasn't as if she had an heir to leave her half to anyway, he'd seen to that. And why should she trust Avi to have her best interest? No, the best thing to do was take the money. So she did. She was finally free to pursue something that had plagued her for over 15 years, and that is what she planned to do.

18

Homework

Eden rode in the front seat of Sterling's car as he drove to his house.

"Oh Sterling, honestly! I feel like you're freaking out for nothing. They're just your parents. Trust me. I know how to behave. Besides, I don't care what they think of me. I am 'poor' as far as your parents are concerned and not good enough to be your friend, so what?"

Eden was trying to convince Sterling that she could handle his parents, he needn't worry.

"I only care what you think, not them."

"I know, but seriously Eden, you can't talk about the Inside, just don't."

"Fine, don't worry, I won't."

Sterling knew this time his father would surely grill Eden with questions about her upbringing and her parents and he wanted her to be evasive, not to lie exactly, but the more his father knew, the worse it would be. Sterling was afraid he'd lose his temper like he used to. For the most part he kept his emotions tightly controlled these days, but he didn't feel confident he could withstand his father's meanness if it was directed toward Eden.

This time when they arrived at the Silver mansion, Rose Silver greeted them in the foyer, giving Eden an awkward hug.

"Darling, I'm so glad you could make it. And Sterling tells me you'll stay for dinner."

"Yes, I plan to, my father said it's ok, and thanks for having me."

"Mom, we need to work on some school stuff for a while, I'm letting Eden use my computer," taking Eden's hand, Sterling began walking toward his room.

The front doors re-opened behind them and Mr. Silver, holding his briefcase and looking sweaty, entered. He was never home this time of day.

"Oh, Eden, you're here. I'm so glad. I hope you'll make yourself at home."

"Thanks, Mr. Silver, Sterling's letting me use his computer. I don't have my own."

"What are you working on, if you don't mind my asking?"

"Just school stuff, but I'd also like to find information about my mother. Sterling probably told you, it's just my father and me. I'm trying to find out if I have any other relatives."

As Eden shared, Sterling screamed silently, "No, Eden, don't share that with him of all people," but he couldn't stop her, it was too late. Mr. Silver looked intrigued and replied,

"I can help you with that, just say the word. I know people who could help you search."

"Ok, I'll let you know," Eden said.

"Dad, we really need to get started, we have a lot of work to do and not a lot of time."

"Please, please, use the office if you want. I'm done with work for the day."

Avarice Silver silently crossed his fingers behind his back and hoped they would do just that.

"Ok Dad, we'll see you for dinner," Sterling just wanted to get away.

"They seem really nice to me," Eden remarked, but even she could sense there might be an ulterior motive for the niceness.

"Let's use the office, then we can work together, and I can check out your library."

Eden was always eager for new reading material and remembered how extensive the book collection in the library, which was connected to the office, appeared.

They sat at the huge conference table and Sterling handed Eden a laptop.

"It's an extra one. You can have it if you need it. Take it home."

"You know I can't take it Inside. The rules won't allow it. I'll just have to do my assignments here, with you." She batted her eyelashes and giggled and smiled at him.

"Oh, bummer, we'll have to hang out more," and he smiled back.

"So what kind of homework do you have?" "Actually none, I'm writing about Inside, sort of a journal, I guess."

"Let me read it when you're done."

"Sure."

Eden began to type and read out loud simultaneously.

Brilliant in its simplicity, Inside is what each individual who experiences it, needs it to be without the chaos and destruction of the Outside world. For some, it may function as a temporary escape. Others think of it as a bridge between this world and the next. While it's impossible to die Inside, time does not stand still. You age normally and time will pass regularly and the things you try to escape will be waiting for you when you return. So why go in? Because sometimes all that happens in life can become too much. People just need a break. People need nature and unfortunately, it's been destroyed, but not Inside. Inside is nature in its purest form, an experience no money or virtual reality can ever buy. Children can almost always get in, but not adults. Once you're an adult, if you go Inside, you have to choose to stay. If you leave, you can't come back.

Eden's voice cracked.

"Sterling, what are you going to choose? After next year, you won't be able to go in and out, only my dad and the Sage can."

"I've thought about it a lot. I could easily stay Inside forever, I love it there. I'd give up all of this, in a heartbeat. I figure I'll stay Outside once I'm of age. You'll still be able to go in and out, and I'll be here, waiting."

Then Eden confided in her friend.

"I think my father is sick, Sterling. I think he's going to die soon. I'm afraid of being alone. He makes me a good person."

"Eden, you are a good person, and you have me. You always will."

Mr. Silver sat in his leather recliner and zoomed in the camera lens for a tight shot of Eden's face and shuddered at the violet eyes. He was looking at his computer screen, watching and recording and listening in on his son and the girl. If there was still an unspoiled place in nature, he wanted to find it. It sounded unbelievable, but the way they were talking made him feel it was indeed real.

Much to Sterling's surprise and relief, his parents did not press Eden for information during dinner. Mr. Silver was not feeling well. Apparently he'd been overcome with shivers, maybe a fever, and didn't want to get anyone else sick. He decided to take his meal in his room. Eden saw no more of him that evening. Sterling's mother joined them and was as polite as she was capable of, prattling on about fashion and other trivial topics.

"Eden, I've been meaning to ask you, who does your hair? I love the color. Is it 'honey flax'? I know that's all the rage these days. I went with 'light ash gold' myself, it's what my stylist recommended for my skin tone," and she fluffed her hair to emphasize her pride in it.

"Mom! That's Eden's real hair. She doesn't color it," Sterling said. His mom could be so shallow.

Rose Sterling ignored the comment and addressed Eden again.

"Just let me know if you ever want to meet my girl. She's a fabulous stylist. She could do wonders for you. Maybe you'd like a facial, or to get your nails done? Anyway, just let me know."

"Um, thanks. I'll do that," Eden said politely while Sterling fumed at his mother's pretentiousness. In her own way, Sterling had to admit, his mother did seem to have a genuine affection for Eden.

Later, when his wife and son were asleep, Mr. Silver got up and padded softly in slippered feet to his office. He sat in the chair where Eden had sat earlier. He noticed a single strand of golden hair stuck to the chair back. He carefully picked it up.

19

The Baby

The day the call came, Celia and Greyson were filled with anticipation. Celia, using her best breathless, pain-filled voice, informed her maid she was going into labor and instructed the woman to tell a few key friends. For the last nine and a half months instead of hiding her fake pregnancy, she'd flaunted it. She made sure all the women knew. Every two weeks she strapped on a bigger fake belly. She wished to have no doubt in anyone's mind that she was about to have a child. She and her husband reserved the hospital suite where she would "recover" for five days before bringing home the baby. They arrived at the hospital and settled in. The little bundle was handed to the Blacks by a nurse. The new parents passed the baby back and forth uncomfortably. Neither had ever held a baby before, and nothing about it felt natural.

"Oh, it's beautiful. What nice golden hair, and a sturdy little thing too," Celia exclaimed.

"Should we wake him up? I want to see those green eyes." She stumbled, correcting herself.

"What I mean to say is I hope he'll have green eyes. Of course we don't know yet."

As far as the nurses were informed, Mrs. Black had just given birth and was in recovery. They had just taken over the last shift. Every precaution was put into place to ensure the privacy of parents who designed their child whether out of necessity or choice.

"We'll call him Greyson Black II of course," Mr. Black proudly stated.

"Um, Sir," the nurse began, but she was promptly interrupted.

"Now nurse, if you could please take him away, we'd like to rest. The nanny will be here tomorrow, and she'll need to be trained. We'll press the buzzer if we need you."

The young nurse walked away cuddling the bundle. She felt sorry for the little one and did not wish to be around when the parents discovered their child might not be exactly what they expected.

For the next few days, the nurses or the nanny would bring the baby to the new parents for a few minutes at a time as Celia Black played the role of a recuperating new mother. On the fourth day, when the Blacks were scheduled to leave the next morning, Celia Black turned to the nurse and asked, "Why is it always sleeping? I'd like to see the child awake for once."

The nurse tenderly stroked the baby's face.

"Wake up little Gracie, wake up, little one."

The baby stirred and opened its eyes. It looked straight up at Celia.

"Those aren't green eyes!" Celia was surprised and more than a little disappointed. She had been adamant about green eyes. Green eyes were unusual and she wanted her child to share this trait with her.

"What color are those eyes? Greyson, come have a look. This child's eyes are strange. They almost look purple, or violet. Is it possible? No one has violet eyes do they?"

Mr. Black responded, "What difference does it make? The eyes can see, can't they? Let's make sure of it. Nurse, have the doctor please verify this child's eyesight."

This nurse, like the others, was new and young and easily intimidated. She did not wish to upset the Blacks. She took the child from Mr. Black, promising to have the doctor check the baby's eyesight.

On the fifth day, the Blacks checked out of the hospital, eager to bring their baby home. The nanny sat next to the child's car seat in the back. She and two others would work eight hour shifts around the clock, their sole duty being the care of the Black's new baby. Once the nannies and baby were settled in, one would hardly know the family had grown. Celia and Greyson Black went on about their normal routine. Celia continued to check in a few times a day to briefly hold the child. She was hoping to feel a surge of love, but she honestly didn't, at least not yet. She only felt an irritating dull ache in her arms and shoulders after she held the child. The doctor warned not to have visitors until two weeks passed. There was a nasty flu going around and the child should be isolated for its own protection.

Celia came alone to the baby's room three days after being home. The nanny was taking a break as the child slept. She noticed a little hand-made sign on the wall near the crib. It said, "Gracie." Celia immediately took it down, grateful her husband hadn't seen it. He would not approve of such a feminine nickname for his son. As she looked over, the baby woke up.

"I can do this," she thought, and she picked up the baby. She stared at those violet eyes. The child squirmed in her arms then retched and vomited all over itself and her. Celia struggled not to drop the child as it wiggled and squirmed. Her arms began to ache again. She shouted for the nanny, feeling instantly nauseous from the smell. She set the baby down on the changing table where it continued to squirm and was now upset and crying. Her first thought was to get out of her own ruined clothes and take a shower, but she couldn't just walk away from the baby.

That would be wrong, wouldn't it? And cruel?

Where was the nanny? Celia shouted for her again. She vaguely remembered the nanny had said she was going for a short walk.

"Don't worry," the nanny had said, "The baby will sleep for at least an hour."

It was then Celia realized she must change the baby herself. Celia set her child on the changing table. She unwrapped the swaddle and proceeded to remove the baby's diaper. Her whole body froze when she saw that her son was not a son, but a daughter. How could this be? There must have been some sort of mix up at the hospital. This was not the child they ordered. Something had gone wrong. Maybe this was why she felt no love for the child, maybe this baby wasn't hers at all. She set the baby in the crib and called her husband.

"Greyson, come home. Something is wrong with the baby."

When Mr. Black arrived home, he found his wife hysterical. She'd had a few drinks and taken some pills to calm her nerves, neither of which had worked. Mr. Black was hardly upset at all. He tried to comfort his wife.

"I'll call the lab and explain. They'll know what to do."

The lab offered no condolences. The head scientist explained, "You signed the papers. We informed you. You don't always get what you order. These are humans."

Mr. Black sat facing his wife.

"So the baby didn't work out. Don't worry dear, we'll order a new one. It didn't have the eyes you wanted anyway, and we don't need a girl. There's no reason to cry about it. Here, have another pill and go to sleep. Just leave this mess to me. I'll fix it. I promise."

"But Grey, how will we explain it? Everyone thinks I had a baby. This is so humiliating, I'll never be able to show my face," Celia continued to sob.

"Honey, this happens all the time. The infant mortality rate is huge. We have nothing to explain. Think of all the attention and sympathy you'll get," Mr. Black soothed.

"But you wouldn't kill the baby would you?" Celia would not condone the killing of a baby, even to save herself some embarrassment. Even Celia was not that cold-hearted.

"No, no, not kill it. I'll find it a home. I'll pay to keep this quiet. No one will ever find out, and we'll try again for our green-eyed son."

"Okay," Celia agreed. "It's not as bad as I thought. I'm exhausted. I ache all over. Maybe I'll sit in the hot tub. No, I think I'll just go to bed." She took yet another pill, one formulated to help provide a long and dreamless sleep. Celia looked forward to putting this mess behind her.

Celia may not have felt as calm as she did if she'd known at the time the little girl was in fact her only chance at having a child. The Blacks hired the scientist again, but due to "circumstances we cannot control," a second child was not to be. The Blacks would remain childless.

20

Campground

"Do you have your car today?" Eden asked Sterling. "I was thinking we could ditch our last three classes and explore the area where my dad grew up."

Eden shared with Sterling all the information she'd learned from her dad and she was eager to try to piece together her past. It was generous of Sterling's father to offer help, but she could tell from his energy, Mr. Silver didn't like her and was only trying to pretend to be cool in front of his son. It didn't work. Sterling could barely tolerate either of his parents and would prefer not involving them at all. He was frustrated that they knew as much as they did about Eden. He felt it was none of their business.

"Excellent, I'm down," Sterling said and together they walked out of Upper School for Adolescents. Their parents would be informed of the truancy of course, but Eden knew her dad would understand just as Sterling knew his parents wouldn't care. Before Eden came to Upper School, he had ditched all the time.

Eden was not embarrassed to admit, she loved riding in Sterling's car and wished she could drive it. Sterling drove to the abandoned campground and parked. It was where with Mitch, he had first entered Inside. That was a day he would never forget. It was definitely in the top three best of his life. He parked in a vacant lot near the train stop. They would walk in as he and Mitch had done, so as not to draw attention to themselves. The pavement in the old parking lot was cracked. A few straggly weeds popped through. Dried out dusty trees hovered around the edges. It was not a place frequented by anyone in recent years.

"We shouldn't be out in this air more than two hours, even with the nose guards," Sterling reminded Eden.

"If we need a break, we can go Inside. We're not too far from one of the entrances." It was the one Sterling used to use.

"Ok. I guess we just start exploring and see what we see. I can't imagine anyone lives here anymore, since the air's unfiltered."

After walking for an hour, following faint trails that looked like they hadn't seen footprints in years, Eden began to feel discouraged.

"I don't know what I thought I was going to find. This was a dumb idea. A person would have to be crazy to live out here."

Since recently learning for sure that she and her father were not blood related, Eden didn't know how she could find out anything about who she really was. No one had turned her into Abandoned Children. If they had, she might be able to find some records. It would seem she just showed up at the camp with Mitch's parents. How did she get there? If only there was someone she could talk to. Tears of disappointment filled her eyes, which she did not attempt to hide from Sterling. He searched for words to comfort her.

"Eden, I know who my parents are, and they're awful, the worst. I'm sure I sound ungrateful, but you've seen. You're lucky to have Mitch, he's probably the best father anyone could ask for. He is the reason I didn't turn into a complete psycho. Believe me, I was not a good kid, until I met you," and he playfully punched her arm. This was their special friendship move. It conveyed the words they couldn't say out loud and it made Eden smile.

"Before we leave, I'm gonna climb this tree and see if I can spot any signs of life." It was a last effort before Eden conceded there was nothing to learn here.

"Boost me up."

Sterling made a step with both hands for Eden and lifted her to the lowest branch of a rather dead-looking tree. She began to climb, then stopped and was about to descend when something caught her eye. It looked like an old structure and it was not far away. She was even more excited to spot what looked like a thin plume of smoke.

"I think I see something," she said as she scrambled down and jumped out of the tree.

"Let's go."

It was definitely a smoldering campfire. If someone wasn't here now, they had been or were still close by.

"Is anyone here?" Eden called. No response.

"Please, we aren't trying to bother you." Eden decided to continue speaking, sure whoever was nearby could hear her voice. What did she have to lose?

"My father's parents used to live here. Their names were Edith and Joe Allbright. They're gone now, but I'm hoping to find someone who knew them, or maybe remembers my father. His name is Mitch."

Eden waited, hoping. She was almost positive she heard rustling in the bushes. She saw an unmistakable shadow move among the trees, then asked, "Did you know them?"

"I'll talk to you," a woman's voice replied. "But, come no closer. I don't want you to see me. I'm bad damaged from being out here. I believe I'm the only one left, and I don't want anyone trying to force me in. I mean to die here, it's where I belong." The woman was elderly and frail and her arthritis kept her in a constant state of pain.

"Thank you." Eden said, "We won't bother you, or tell anyone you're here. Trust me. We only have some questions."

"I knew the Allbrights. They were your kin you say?"

"Yes, my grandparents. My dad lived here with them when he was a boy, and then he left."

"Then your father was little Mitch."

"Yes."

"He was a good boy. I always thought this was no place for a child. I was glad when he left for school. You know, I think his parents meant well. They were good folks. Some of us just aren't meant to live in society. We don't like bein' told what to do. That's why we had our own little community here. And when people were forced into the buildings, 'for their own protection', we chose not to go. You understand me?" she asked.

"Yes, I get it," Eden said, "I don't like being forced to do anything either."

"What I need to know is if you ever remember the Allbrights having a baby, besides Mitch I mean."

"Let me think on it." The woman paused for a moment. "Can't say as I do."

It was impossible for Eden to hide her disappointment.

"Oh, okay. I guess that's all. Thanks for letting us talk to you. We won't bother you anymore."

Eden and Sterling both concluded that it seemed to be a dead end, but just as they started to walk away, the voice spoke again.

"There was babies sometimes though, but they wasn't theirs. There was a girl child. Joe brought her home. It wasn't uncommon. Some rich person would offer to pay one of us to take a baby, bring it here to raise for a while and then turn it in. Never did it myself. They didn't want to send their unwanteds to Abandoned Children, always afraid it could be traced to them. Usually they were designers, the babies."

"Designers? What's a designer?" Eden wasn't sure she'd heard correctly.

Sterling definitely was familiar with the term but hadn't ever heard it used so casually. It was one of those things that adults whispered about or they used the term to insult someone else. The woman's voice continued, "Some of them rich folks can't have kids so they create them in a lab. None of them want to admit it. It's all very secret. Sometimes what they order, is not what they get. Occasionally, over the years, I've seen some of them children end up here. They never stay for long. Like I said, this ain't no place for a child, and so after a while the children were taken to Abandoned Children, but by then they couldn't be traced."

"You said the Allbrights had a girl child. Do you know where Joe got her? Where she came from?" Sterling asked.

"Joe Allbright sometimes worked in the Black and Silver Estates compound, where all the rich people live. He was good at gardening, you know, landscaping. He'd work a while then go back when he ran out of money. It wasn't a regular job. I believe they call them day laborers. He probably got her from there, got paid to take her away."

Both Sterling and Eden found they were holding their breath. Immediately Sterling tried to think of all the possibilities within the compound, including the most frightening possibility of all, his own parents. Afraid that she might stop speaking to them, neither wanted to interrupt the woman, but Eden had to ask.

"Do you remember anything else about the baby?"

"Some of them babies, they wasn't quite right. Makes sense don't it? I mean why else would they get rid of them? It sure can't be cheap to make one. That baby seemed fine. Could be she wasn't wanted just for bein' a girl. Course everyone wanted a son. Also, coulda' been them eyes. The baby had unusual eyes, like a purple color. I remember someone in camp here started a rumor that the baby was a dark child, an evil child, said she'd bring us all trouble. You know how rumors are, don't you? Soon people start to believe them. They sure didn't have that baby long, must've taken her to Abandoned Children, I don't know for sure. That's a long time ago."

"I'm the baby," Eden said. Her voice was shaky. It was a lot to take in.

"Mitch, my dad, came back to visit his parents and I was here. He was only nineteen himself, but he didn't want to leave me."

"Well, I'm sure I don't have nothin' else to tell you then, except it's best he took you. You know, the Allbrights, both of them died not too long after that," the woman said.

Sterling and Eden thanked the woman. She remained hidden in the shadows, but Eden stepped closer to the voice and said, "Please may I just shake your hand? You've really helped me."

The tiny woman held out her curled, arthritic hand, keeping her face shielded in shadow. Eden touched it very gently saying, "Thank you," one more time.

"I'm just going to leave you some money. We're so grateful for your help." Sterling set down some money and he and Eden walked back toward the car. During the ride, each was lost in thought, not sure what to do or say about what they had just learned.

When she was certain they were gone, the old lady came out of the shadows to collect the money Sterling left. Oddly, her fingers uncurled and moved with ease. In fact, her whole body was pain free.

21

The Solution

As much as he would have preferred to take care of the matter alone, Greyson Black enlisted the help of his partner and friend Avarice Silver. They met at the office and he explained the situation. Knowing Avi was not above shady business dealings, he figured the man might have a quick solution to the "problem" of the designer baby gone wrong.

Sure enough, he did.

The solution involved paying one of the day laborers to take the baby away, keep it for a while, then turn it in to Abandoned Children as if it was the laborer's own child. This plan seemed simple and straightforward, particularly if they chose one of those people still too stubborn to move into housing, insisting on staying out in the poisonous air, there would be little chance of being found out. Those people did not want attention, but would be glad to earn some extra money for their silence and an easy job.

Mr. Silver carefully selected a man who sometimes did gardening projects at the Black and Silver Estates. The man was glad to accept a sum so large he would not have to work again for quite some time. He agreed to take the child and keep her for a month or so. He was to claim he and his sick wife were unable to care for her, when they turned the child in.

It was a simple, fail-safe plan.

The two businessmen met the gardener at the entrance to an old campground outside of town. The man said he lived nearby with his wife. The men did not press for specifics, they didn't want to know. The baby was in the backseat of the car wrapped in a blanket. Neither thought to strap her in or sit in the backseat with her to keep her safe. It was easier if they didn't think of her as a child, but as an experiment gone wrong.

Mr. Silver was cold. He kept turning up the heat, but couldn't seem to warm up. His whole body felt chilled and he wondered if he wasn't coming down with something. Mr. Black was not cold, but quiet on the drive, thankful for the solution, yet plagued with some guilt which he kept pushing out of his mind.

The deep chill grew worse as Mr. Silver lifted the baby from the back seat, holding her in one hand and the money in the other. The terms of the arrangement were reviewed once more before the final exchange. As he handed her over, the baby looked up and locked eyes with Avarice Silver for a quick second. Shivering, he addressed the man who was willing to take the child, one final time.

"Well, thanks for doing business with us. Remember, do not contact either of us for any reason. Ever. This is your responsibility now."

With that, Mr. Silver handed the man an additional roll of money, more than the poor man had ever seen before. Mr. Silver and Mr. Black got into the car and drove away as the stranger, holding the child, disappeared into the night.

Neither man in the car looked back.

"It'll be fine. Right?" Mr. Black thought aloud.

"Of course, Grey. I am so cold. I think I'm getting sick."

The shivering was worse as they entered the Black and Silver Compound. Mr. Silver parked.

"I'll see you at the office tomorrow, Avi, and thanks again," Mr. Black said as he opened the car door.

"Don't worry about it buddy. You'd have done the same for me, partner." He clapped him on the back.

As he entered his house, Mr. Silver buzzed for the cook. "I need a hot brandy. I am freezing. Bring it to me in the hot tub, and be quick about it."

"Of course, Mr. Silver," and the cook went about her orders.

At the Black's house, Celia Black hadn't left her room since her breakdown. Her husband kept checking on her, and each time fed her more pills. The arrangement planned by Mr. Black and Mr. Silver, was completed. The child was given away and life could go on as before in the Black household. The news leaked out that the Black's child had died. Celia and Greyson Black received flowers and notes of sympathy from friends in their social circle. When Celia finally made an appearance, she looked the part of a grieving mother, and respectfully, just as her husband predicted, no one pressed her for details of the tragedy.

Only Avarice Silver knew the truth. He delivered a large sum of money to the scientist responsible for creating the baby and asked only that it not happen again. By accepting the money, the scientist agreed never to create another child for Celia and Greyson Black. The money was a good faith offering accompanied by an outright threat of exposure if the scientist were ever to go back on his promise. And with this, there would be one heir and one heir only with claim to the Black and Silver Empire, his son, Sterling Silver. When the time was right, he would help his son choose a proper and suitable wife and the family line would continue.

22

Gemma

Other than Conversation class, Eden thought it best to keep to herself. Even in Conversation, she and Sterling preferred to sit alone. Today the instructor had more specific directions.

"I feel most of you have mastered small talk, so we are moving on to other topics of interest. I'd like you to pair up and choose a student you don't know well."

Ember practically threw herself in Sterling's lap, avoiding eye contact with Eden.

"Let's be partners, Sterling. We hardly know each other." She nuzzled up to him and cooed.

"Um, sure, fine." Sterling wasn't thrilled.

Eden stood to look for someone who didn't yet have a partner.

"You can stay with me." Sterling didn't want her to leave.

"No, I'll pair up with the girl over there. I'm good. But, thanks." She gave him a playful punch on the arm.

Eden looked right at Ember.

"Behave yourself. Oh, and I'm glad your little skin problem cleared up."

Eden strode over and sat in an empty chair next to a girl she recognized, but hadn't ever spoken to. Her skin was dark, her eyes almond shaped, and she was petite like Eden.

"Hi, I'm Gemma," the girl greeted her warmly. She extended her hand and Eden shook it. She could tell this was a genuine girl and she relaxed, glad to introduce herself.

"I'm Eden."

"I know. Everybody knows who you are." There was no malice; she was just stating a fact.

"Why does everybody know me?" Eden found this interesting.

"You're new. You're beautiful. You're Sterling's girlfriend," Gemma answered.

"True. Thanks. We're just friends though, best friends." Eden responded smiling. It was amusing how every girl seemed interested in Sterling.

The instructor gave the directions for the day's experience.

"Ok, so today I want you to learn about the person you are paired up with, not about their virtual life, about their real life and interests. It's important to know how to have a real conversation and get to know someone. As we use technology more and more, I fear this is a skill that is sometimes forgotten, though it's not unimportant. I want you to talk about three different things, family, home life, or a hobby. Hobbies involving technology are off-limits. Ready......go."

"You first," Eden said.

"I'd like to know about your family. I don't have a mother, so I'd like to know about yours."

So Gemma began.

"I live a pretty boring life compared to some of the others at Upper. I have a mom and dad and six siblings, and we're commoners." Gemma prepared for the shocked face, but Eden didn't look shocked, she just waited patiently to hear more. So Gemma continued.

"I know that's not typical, no one has six kids. My siblings are all adopted. I'm my parents' only biological child. We grow a lot of our food. We don't have a nanny or a maid. My mom teaches the younger kids at home. She got approval because she specialized as a teacher in school. My dad's a maintenance worker. We have two dogs and three cats. It's pretty crowded, but fun. We don't really have anything fancy, it's just a simple apartment, under one of the domes, just outside the city. I don't know. I like it. I guess I'm happy. I wouldn't change it. I'm here at Upper because I'm bright, smart."

Gemma hadn't ever spoken so much at school. At home she was a regular chatterbox, but at school she kept to herself. It felt so good to talk about her life and her family, she just wished she didn't have to feel like she needed to defend her upbringing. It was so different from most of the other students at Upper School.

"It sounds," Eden searched for words, "really wonderful." There was no trace of sarcasm in her voice, she was sincere and Gemma could tell and was relieved.

"I've never shared that with anyone here."

"Well, thanks. I think you'll find we have more in common than you expected."

It was Eden's turn to share. She told Gemma about the place where she grew up and how until this year, she'd spent her life there. She described it and assured her it was not virtual, but a real place, how it was simple and communal and the people were honest. She spoke of Vita, her best girlfriend. It felt good to describe it. Eden felt proud. And for the first time, besides Sterling, she felt she might have a friend Outside.

23

The Journal

Celia Black strode right past the receptionist and knocked quickly on the heavy office door before pushing it open and entering, not waiting to be invited in. Avarice Silver looked up and was surprised to find her there.

"Celia, what brings you here today?"

Celia tried to contain her emotions. She wanted to be forceful, but not rude. She especially did not want to cry, out of anger or frustration. She hoped her rehearsal in the mirror beforehand would help. She wasn't used to confrontation and often found her thoughts became jumbled.

"Avi, I want to find the child, the one we gave away. It was a mistake. I don't know what I was thinking back then. What can you tell me?"

Avarice Silver looked her straight in the eyes.

"Celia, I don't know what you mean. Didn't your son die?"

She knew then, he was going to deny it.

"Look, I don't want to play games. I just want any information you can give me. I know that you know. You and

Grey took care of it. What did you do? Do you know where she is now?”

Avarice decided to bluff, unsure how much Celia actually knew. What had Grey told her? They swore secrecy and he hadn’t been close to his wife. Maybe Celia was simply looking for information.

“I’m sorry, I don’t know what you’re talking about.” He paused and tried his best at sympathy.

“Celia, you’re stressed. You’re clearly still grieving over Grey’s death. It’s understandable. What you need is to get away. I’ll ask Marta to book a vacation for you; she’ll know what’s best.” He stood and leaned forward calling out to his receptionist, dwarfing Celia, who was now sitting in a chair. He shouted over her head, “Marta, Marta, book a trip for Celia. Do it now. And get Rose’s doctor on the phone. Make Celia an appointment. And please turn up the heat, it’s freezing in here!”

Celia’s voice was rising as she responded.

“I don’t need any appointments or trips! Avi, I know everything. And no, Grey never told me, even though I asked many times. I know because I’ve been going through his stuff, rearranging, redecorating. I cleaned out his office. I’d like to make myself a spa salon in that room. It’s a gorgeous room. It’s got great light. It's perfect for a salon. I saw a picture of how it should look. Grey had a lot of old papers. I told the maids to shred it all. What do I need it for? He was always a pack rat.”

Celia's thoughts seemed to jump around. She was agitated and Avi wondered if she'd taken too many pills today. He feigned concern, lightly patting her shoulder. She pulled away, recoiling from his touch and continued.

"Don't distract me. I'm in charge now. As I was saying.....what was I saying?"

"You shredded his paperwork and are taking over his home office for a spa, right?"

"Yes, yes. Well, one of the girls, a maid, found a book, a journal of sorts and she gave it to me. I was going to pitch it with everything else and then I thought, 'why not read it?' I was curious to see what my darling late husband wrote about me." Celia wiped an imaginary tear as she sighed for effect.

"And..?" Avarice Silver was not at all sure he liked the direction of this conversation.

"Oh honestly, let's not play games. Aside from his deepest thoughts regarding how much he loved me, he also wrote in detail about the two of you giving the child away."

Mr. Silver sighed long and deep.

"Then you already know. What is it you want from me?" Mr. Silver was growing impatient as well as uneasy, but was hiding it well.

"I expect you to help me find her. Hire someone for me."

"I can help you. Sure Celia, I'll help. I guess I just don't understand what you want from this. Why now? It has to be what, fifteen years ago?"

"We wanted a child so badly, our green-eyed son. Instead we got a girl, and I didn't think I could love her. I thought it'd be easy to try again, get it right. But, thanks to you, we never did."

"What do you mean saying, 'Thanks to me'? What does it have to do with me?" Mr. Silver was confident there was no way Celia could know his involvement. Still, why would she say such a thing?

"I know Avi. I know." Her shrill voice was rising now.

"It was you. You paid the scientist to never create another child for us. We kept trying time and time again, spending loads of money, and he couldn't give an explanation, just said it happens sometimes. Grey wrote in his journal he suspected you had a hand in it, but he never confronted you. I contacted the scientist and he admitted it. What does he care now? He's on his deathbed anyway. He confirmed it. So, as I see it, I have at least two convictable crimes I could turn you in for. You'd be humiliated and jailed, and as much as I'd kind of like that for what you did, I won't turn you in, as long as you help me."

Mr. Silver thought fast. It was a skill he'd honed over the years and it was what made him so successful.

"What was the year of the journal entries Celia?"

"I'm not sure. Why?"

"Well, because not too long ago Grey did confront me about the scientist."

This was a lie.

"And I did admit to paying him, and I apologized."

This too was a lie.

"And I helped Grey learn what happened to the girl child."

Still another lie. Mr. Silver was on a roll and was very convincing.

Dishonesty and greed are two of man's greatest flaws, and Avarice Silver possessed them both in abundance.

"I don't believe a word of this Avi," but in truth, Celia was doubtful and Mr. Silver detected a slight waver in her voice. He knew she was losing her confidence. He struck back with…

"Consider that Grey never told you, because he didn't like what we found. He didn't want to upset you."

"What? What did you find?" Now Celia was definitely panicked.

"Perfect," thought Mr. Silver and he explained, complete with an appropriate grave expression.

"The child is dead, Celia."

Here he paused for dramatic effect.

"She was never turned in at Abandoned Children because she died. I'm sorry, but that is the honest truth. I would never lie to you."

Mr. Silver stood then, indicating the conversation was over. He put on his coat and called his receptionist on the intercom.

"Marta, please turn up the heat and did you book something for Celia?"

Marta's voice came through the speaker.

"Sir, it is 80 degrees in your office. You want the heat up higher?"

"Yes, turn it up. I must be getting sick, I can't get warm."

Celia stood to leave. She didn't seem too disappointed at the news, and as far as Mr. Silver could tell, she believed him. Hopefully it would not come up again.

"I'll talk to Marta about a vacation. I guess I could use a get-away," she said.

"Yes, you really should, absolutely. You know Grey would want you to enjoy yourself. I can't wait to see the spa room. Give me a ring when that's done. I don't think anyone in the whole complex has her own spa room. All the ladies will be so jealous of you, especially Rose. Maybe I shouldn't tell her or she'll want one too."

By the time she walked out of his office, Celia was all smiles and could think of nothing but the envious looks on the faces of the other ladies. And just like that, her long lost child was forgotten once again.

Avi left the office early, still unable to get warm and now feeling quite ill. He needed to speak with his son. As he drove home, he thought about the night, so long ago, when he'd helped his friend deal with the problem of the unwanted baby.

What he'd told Celia was largely a lie, but there was a grain of truth too. A few years back he actually had gone and checked all the records at Abandoned Children and no girl child was surrendered during the year in question, or during the four years after that. It was as if the baby he helped Greyson Black give away, had vanished. As he explained to Celia, he was certain the baby must have died. He still wanted to believe it, desperately wanted to believe it. Upon arriving home, he went to his office, closed the door behind him, and made the call to the lab. It was time to get the information he needed.

"I'm calling about the samples I sent you. Yes, sample numbers 589372 and 589373. I need to know if they match." He held his breath, but knew the answer even before the technician responded.

"Yes sir. We have an 85% match. That's typical for a Designer. Is there anything else."

"No, no thank you." Mr. Silver hung up the phone. His hands were shaking, and he was overcome with dread.

<u>24</u>

A Plan

Sterling noticed he was seeing more of his father lately. Too much for his taste. Here was a man who never took any interest in his life, suddenly ever-present it seemed. Sterling suspected the reason. He would soon finish at Upper School and his father would have a plan for what was expected of him next. Today he'd messaged Sterling to come straight home after school. He wished to have a meeting in the office.

"Whose dad requests a formal 'meeting' with him?" Sterling joked with Eden.

"Sounds serious," she'd said. "Tell me about it tomorrow. I think I'll ride the train with Gemma. I really like her."

Avarice Silver had one thought and one thought alone as he followed Eden that afternoon. It was, "she must die". He wasn't sure how to do it. She was with another girl today, clearly a commoner. Avi was skilled at identifying those he felt were beneath him. He needed to get Eden alone, no witnesses. It should look like an accident even though an inquiry would be unlikely. No resources would be wasted on figuring out how a young girl died, especially if it were to appear as if by her own hand. Yes, if it was deemed a suicide he could even provide a tearful testimony of how she'd loved his son and that love was unrequited. It would work, no question, and he could get on with his life.

Every fiber in his body warned him the girl was dangerous, greedy, and worse, seemed intelligent. It was as if he recognized his own unsavory qualities in another and it frightened him. If she ever found out her true identity he was certain she would ruin him and his son and the empire he had built. Why wouldn't she? She came from nothing, and they had everything. He never wanted to look at those unsettling violet eyes again.

"My son, I can handle," he thought. It was with some regret Mr. Silver realized he didn't know his own son, but he felt fairly certain his only child would listen to the voice of reason, after the girl was out of the way and no longer a constant distraction. Sterling enjoyed his life of privilege, and surely wouldn't risk it over a silly crush. Until now the boy was an accessory in his father's life, but as he was nearing adulthood, it was time their relationship changed. Yes, he would bring him into the business, teach him all he knew and together they would expand the Silver Empire he had built.

As Eden stepped forward to board the train, Mr. Silver was overcome with the urge to push her onto the tracks. It would be quick and easy, but ultimately too risky. Someone might see. He would need to hire a person to do it for him, and it should look like an accident. No, not today, but soon, he thought. He rushed home, trying to beat Sterling. This was going to be a hard conversation.

Sterling and his father arrived at almost exactly the same time. Sterling thought his father looked rushed, as he always did, and stressed out.

"Hey Dad, I'm gonna just grab a snack. Did you still want to talk to me?"

"Yes, meet me in my office. We'll talk there."

Sterling poured himself some cereal, not bothering to wait for the cook. He balanced it in one hand, and headed to his father's office. He felt uneasy, something told him he was not going to enjoy this, "talk."

Mr. Silver was behind the desk, looking intimidating. Sterling sat opposite his father, his lean youthful frame slouching defiantly in the chair, and heartily dug into his cereal.

"Can we make this quick? I have homework," he asked with a mouthful of cereal and a trace of boredom.

This set his dad off. Mr. Silver had planned to stay calm and collected, but his son's cavalier attitude infuriated him. They were so unalike, he thought.

"Sit up straight, Boy. Since you're in such a hurry, I'll get right to the point. I forbid you to see the girl again. There. That's it. You're excused." Mr. Silver waved him off. Sterling laughed sarcastically in his father's face.

"You can't forbid me to do anything. I'll spend time with who I like."

"You won't. She's dangerous. You have no idea who she is, what she's capable of."

"I know more than you think," Sterling shot back with rising anger.

"I know she's a designer. I just don't know who created her."

His father, caught off guard, just stared. The vein in his temple began to bulge and pulse.

"Oh my God! Was it you? Did you create her? And get rid of her?" Sterling felt sick to his stomach as he finally voiced this possibility aloud.

"No. No, not me, but I know who did. They got rid of her because she was... wrong."

Avarice Silver wondered to himself. *How in the world does Sterling know this much?*

"It was the Blacks, Greyson and Celia. They did it," he blurted out.

May as well take the blame off himself.

"Son, if she finds out who she is, she could ruin me, ruin us."

"She never would. Dad, I know her."

Mr. Silver wanted his son to fear the girl as he did.

"You don't know the power she has. Look, I don't expect you to believe me, but she's powerful, she can harm people, inflict pain, cause things to happen. She's evil. That's why they got rid of her. She's evil, trust me."

"Trust you? Are you kidding me?"

Sterling knew Eden was powerful. Eden knew it too. She sometimes made things happen by accident, when she was hurt or angry. Sterling also knew he loved her, more than he had ever loved anyone, or could love anyone, and he knew he would protect her. He needed to figure out what his father had in mind. He would put nothing past him, the man had no scruples.

"I'd better play along," Sterling thought.

"So what should we do Dad, if she's so dangerous?" Sterling pretended to come around to his father's way of thinking.

"First of all, stay away from her. She'd be just the type to get pregnant, then try to blame it on you and get money from me."

Sterling was furious.

"How many times do I have to tell you we're just friends? She's only 15. You don't understand, probably because you have no friends, only enemies."

His father acted as if he hadn't heard a word.

"Son, there's only one solution. Don't you worry about it. I'll take care of everything." His voice trailed off, "I know people..."

Sterling then locked eyes with his father. He too, had power, it was the power to bend people to his will, whether by physical force or mental, and it rarely failed him. He'd been using it all his life. The only person who seemed immune was his father, and until now, it hadn't mattered. Hadn't his parents seen to it that his every desire was catered to as a child?

Sterling leaned in close to his father, right in his face and said, "If you harm a single hair on Eden's head, I will kill you. Do you hear me? I will kill you!" He stood abruptly, knocking over the chair, and stomped out the door.

The tone in his voice told the man his son was serious. Mr. Silver knew then that he would need to plan carefully. He called after Sterling.

"Okay, Son, calm down, we'll figure this out. No one's killing anyone."

Sterling was not reassured, not at all. He found his mother in her dressing room, where she sat relaxing, her face covered in cream.

"Oh, Sterling, you're alone, right? I wouldn't want anyone to see me so indisposed."

"Yeah, I'm alone. Mom, I need to talk to you about Dad. I'm worried. He's lost it. He's completely crazy."

"Oh, Sterling, you always were dramatic, what is it?"

"Mom, focus. Dad wants to kill Eden. Seriously, he does. He told me."

"You're so silly. I don't know what's gotten into you, but that's not funny, Sterling."

Sterling wondered if he should keep trying to get through to his mother, but decided it was a waste of time.

"Okay, Mom. I guess I'll see you later."

"Sure, Sweetheart."

<u>25</u>

An Accident

At Upper School, preparations were in full swing. Sterling and the other senior level students were preparing to graduate. Most were from wealthy families and would never have to worry about making a living. Still, all participated in a battery of tests designed to figure out where they were most gifted, so they could choose to use their talents, or not. Sterling hoped for inspiration. He felt most drawn to working with kids, troubled students, like Mitch had worked with him. Sterling seemed to have a knack for reading people and knowing how to help. He could also use his powers of persuasion to get people to do what he wanted, and he could choose to direct it for good. Unfortunately, "counselor" was not a career choice suitable for someone of his rank. It was a middle class job meant for a commoner. He could imagine the incredulous looks on his parents' faces if he told them he planned to make a life of helping others.

Working with his father was the least appealing of all his prospects and he felt a tinge of guilt for his ungratefulness, at least he had a father.

He and Eden had come to terms with the fact that her father was dying. It wouldn't be long. Lately, Mitch had been saying his goodbyes Inside. Everyone knew he would not stay long. When he went Outside again, it would be the last time. Sterling thought Mitch was waiting for Eden to come to terms with it; he was giving her time. Everyone believed Mitch would move forward when he passed on and left them, but it still hurt knowing he wouldn't be around in person.

What Sterling wanted more than anything was to live Inside permanently. There he would be equal with everyone and he could contribute his share. Living Inside would allow him to breathe freely and enjoy real nature. His wealth wouldn't be an issue. He would give it up. Giving it up would be easy, he thought, and a relief. He often daydreamed of living in one of the little burres, sharing meals with the others and meditating in the lodge. He longed for a simple life.

After the last confrontation with his father, they'd rarely spoken. Sterling never brought Eden home, unless he was sure not to run into his father. His mother, as always, remained blissfully unaware of the conflict between her husband and son. Sterling wanted to spend as much time as he could Inside. His birthday was approaching and once it passed he'd have only one more chance to enter, and once in, if he left, he couldn't come back.

Today, Eden was going to Gemma's house and Sterling, feeling just a bit jealous for having not been invited, planned to drive straight home. He watched the girls walk out. They were headed for the station. He saw a black car pull away from the curb. Something was familiar about it. It looked like one of his father's many cars. He strained to see who was driving and it was no one he recognized. Still, he decided to follow Eden. He didn't want her to see him, he'd have to explain and she might think he was jealous. He felt weird, like a stalker, but something nagged at him to follow her. With no time to get his own car, he proceeded on foot. Was he being paranoid? It really seemed like the black car was purposely driving slow, keeping a distance, but tracking the girls.

The girls were just a block away from the station. Sterling felt certain now that the car was following them. He got a sick feeling in the pit of his stomach and quickened his steps. He remembered his father's words, "Don't worry, I'll take care of everything. I know people."

Sterling began to run, but he was still almost a block away. He shouted to Eden, but the velocity of the trains made it impossible for her to hear. His voice just carried off. He willed himself to push harder, run faster. Eden was stepping off the curb. The car picked up speed. Sterling arrived behind her, screaming her name. She never heard him. She never saw him. He pushed her with all his strength, sending her flying across the street where her head hit the cement. The driver slammed on the brakes, but not in time. Sterling was hit almost full force and was thrown forward and then back onto the curb. The black car never stopped. Gemma stood shocked, not believing what she'd just witnessed. There were only a few others around and they all called in the emergency.

The first emergency vehicle to arrive took Sterling, the technicians lifting him out of a growing pool of his own blood. He would go straight to the best hospital, while Gemma sat crying on the dirty pavement, cradling her friend's head in her lap.

"Please be okay, Eden. Please be okay, Eden. Please be okay, Eden."

Eden opened her eyes as she regained consciousness. Her body felt battered, but nothing felt broken. She stood up, and was dizzy, but tried not to show it.

"Eden, don't stand, you're hurt. We need to wait for the next emergency vehicle."

"No, Gemma. I need to get out of here, I don't feel safe. Let's go."

A bystander approached and Eden halted her with a look.

They continued to the station and boarded the train.

"I'll come home with you, Eden. You shouldn't be alone," Gemma said.

"You can't, Gemma, your parents will worry and there's no way to contact them if you come Inside. I'll be fine. I promise. I'm tough. I just have to ask you. What happened back there?" Eden asked.

"I don't really know. It was so fast. You stepped off the curb and it seemed like Sterling appeared out of nowhere. The next thing I knew you were on the other side of the street and I think a car hit Sterling. I don't want to upset you, but there was so much blood, Eden, so much blood."

Gemma began to shake and cry as she re-lived it all again.

"I don't want to leave you either, Gemma, but I need to get home. My Dad will worry and he's really sick." Eden was torn and unsure what to do. Her head throbbed and she couldn't get her thoughts straight. Her friend reassured her.

"Go Eden. You should go home. I'll be fine. You're the one who's hurt. I'll see you tomorrow at school, or maybe in a few days. I think you need to recover. I'll have my parents call the hospital to check on Sterling, but, oh shoot, I won't be able to tell you what's going on. This is when I wish we weren't the only two humans on Earth without a device."

Eden wrapped her friend in a hug, she was grateful for her.

She jumped off the train at the next exit and called out, "I'll see you soon. Seriously, don't worry about me."

As she walked from the station to the closest entrance to Inside, Eden tried to replay what happened, but her thoughts were too fuzzy. She was worried about Sterling, but knew he would have the best possible care. His parents would see to that.

When Eden arrived home, Vita found her and told her to come to the lodge. Mitch was saying goodbye officially. Eden wanted to lie down, the fatigue threatened to overwhelm her, but this was more important.

"It's today? He's really leaving? When is he leaving? I'm not ready for this."

"Well, he's saying goodbye and soon he'll cross over. It's time. He's been warning us, preparing us for weeks. Haven't you been paying attention?"

Eden knew it should be a time to celebrate. No one doubted that Mitch would move forward. Everyone seemed happy for him, but she didn't want him to leave. Who would be her anchor? He was the only father she'd ever known. Eden had two close friends, Vita and Gemma, and she thought she had Sterling too, but she needed to process what happened today. Now she had a splitting headache and felt like she needed to lie down and sleep. She was dizzy too. She wanted her dad more than ever. She needed him all to herself, but how could she pull him away from everyone else?

Eden decided she would find Mitch later. Instead, she sought the Sage. He told her to go to his burre and he would meet her soon. Eden's vision was blurry. She walked slowly to the Sage's burre. It seemed to take forever. Eden entered and spotted a box by the fire pit and without thinking, she opened it. In it were wooden rings of various sizes. She knew these were made by the Sage for the people Inside. Each was unique, designed only to fit the wearer and once placed, never to be removed. Eden looked down at her own ring. It was placed on her finger when she was only an infant, yet it remained a perfect fit. Beneath the rings she spotted a faded photograph. Eden carefully pulled it out and examined it. The boy in the picture reminded her of Sterling, the posture, the facial structure, the dark hair.

"It's me as a boy," the Sage said. He'd come in quietly and Eden hadn't noticed.

"It reminds me of Sterling," Eden said and as she did, she hoped with all she had that Sterling was okay.

"I've noticed that too," the Sage replied.

"I'm worried about my dad, about being without him. I'm worried about Sterling. He's hurt and I just left him. I'm so confused," Eden confessed.

"Your father will be fine, it's his time."

The Sage too, was sorry Mitch would leave. He'd known for a while that Mitch was not his successor, but he had chosen not to dwell on it. His own time was nearing too and at present, he was without a clear successor.

"Eden, I'll take you to Sterling tomorrow. I should go with you. I don't want you going alone. Tonight you need to spend time with your father, he leaves in the morning. Spend this precious time with him."

Eden thanked the Sage, then went to the burre she shared with her dad to wait for him.

Eden and Mitch sat up most of the night by the fire as they had so many times.

"Will I be okay without you, Dad?" Eden wanted to know.

"I couldn't be more proud of you, Eden. Whenever you miss me, come sit by this fire, or if you're Outside, remember me with a donut." He chuckled.

"I love you so much. We'll be together again on the other side one day, I'll be waiting for you, but you're not finished here yet. I am. I must go."

In the morning, at first light, the entire Inside population rose early and gathered to watch Mitch leave them forever. He forbade sadness. Mitch turned and exited the same way he'd come those many years before, and then he disappeared into the light, leaving nothing behind but a deep sense of serenity and peace among the people. It was that simple.

26

Light & Dark

In his hospital bed, under the care of the best doctors money could buy, Sterling was wavering in and out of consciousness. His skull was cracked, and his brain swollen. The doctor leaned over and examined him remarking, "We won't know much till the swelling subsides. Has he spoken at all?" One of the nurses on watch responded.

"He's said 'Eden' a couple of times. Does the name sound familiar? Is she a friend of his?"

"Yes," Mrs. Silver said, choking back her sobs. "Eden is his only friend. We need to find her. I know my darling boy will wake up for Eden."

"There's a girl in the waiting area with a strange old man. Sorry, I shouldn't say strange, but you'll see what I mean. Should I let them in, Mrs. Silver?"

The nurse was aware of the importance of this patient and was willing to bend the rules about non-family member visitors, if it could be beneficial for the patient's recovery. Mrs. Silver, like the nurse, assumed it was Eden waiting, probably with her father. She agreed to let them in. Eden greeted the boy's mother, then went straight to him.

The Sage was surprised.

Never have I felt more energy as I did right then. The atmosphere was charged. As I saw the two young people together, the prophecy started to come into focus.

In bed lay the unconscious boy. Eden touched him and he stirred. His head was bandaged, obscuring his face, but even in this battered state, he was an undeniably beautiful human. Eden rested her head on the pillow with Sterling, her golden hair mingling with his black hair.

The light and the dark...

Eden and the Sage were only there a few minutes before Mr. Silver pushed through the door carrying two hot coffees. He was grumpy because he'd been made to fetch the coffee himself. The nurses informed him this was not their job, and his wife, he knew, was not capable of this complicated task. He nearly spilled them both when he spied Eden, her head resting on Sterling's pillow, her hand holding his. Their closeness unnerved him.

"Who let her in?" he barked. "I said, 'No visitors!,' Someone is getting fired for this."

The Sage stood to the side and watched him grab Eden's arm and roughly escort her out. He knew she could take care of herself, but he had no idea what would unfold. Avarice Silver did not see the Sage there at all. He couldn't. Nor did he see the Sage follow him out and stand by Eden's side as he lied to her.

"Look girl. Are you dim? Sterling isn't interested in you. He tried to push you into oncoming traffic. He wants you gone. The least you can do is disappear from his life. Let him heal, then stay away, or I'll make you stay away. Believe me."

Eden put her face right up close to Mr. Silver's and gave him a hard shove in the chest. He tried not to flinch. He avoided her eyes.

"You know very well, Mr. Silver, you can't make me do anything."

She turned and addressed the Sage. "Isn't that right? Tell him."

Mr. Silver shivered in spite of himself.

"Who are you speaking to? I knew you were crazy, crazy and dangerous. I'm telling you girl, stay away from Sterling, he doesn't want you, and, and, and stay away from our family too. You are not welcome," he hissed and sputtered at her through clenched teeth.

Just then, Rose Silver popped her head out of the door and chirped, "Is everything okay out here?"

"Fine Mrs. Silver, we were just leaving," Eden said, and she and the Sage walked away.

"Who is 'we'?" Mr. Silver wanted to know.

"The old man, he must be Eden's father, or grandfather," Rose answered.

"There was no old man!" Mr. Silver shouted and he wanted to argue, but he was too tired and too cold. He needed that coffee. He removed one of the blankets from his son's bed and slumped exhausted in a fold-out chair.

Sterling was waking now and the first thing he said was, "Where's Eden? I could have sworn I felt her here with me." Mr. Silver pushed up close to the bed, but Mrs. Silver spoke to their son first.

"Oh, she was just here, she just left." It did not occur to Mrs. Silver to try to catch up to Eden.

"Yes, Son. She was here and I sent her away. Do you not remember what happened? She pushed you into traffic. She could've killed you." Mr. Silver hoped his son's head injury would allow him to believe this lie, but Mrs. Silver wasn't having it.

"Oh Avi, what are you talking about? Eden did no such thing, she's his friend."

"Well, I told her never to speak to you again, to go back where she came from, and she completely agreed. She won't bother you again, Son. It's time you found some suitable friends. I can help with that." He was desperate now.

Mr. Silver pressed the call button to summon the doctor, and when the doctor arrived, he demanded more medication for Sterling.

"The boy needs to sleep. Can't you see how agitated he is? Put him out."

"I do not need medication. You're delusional!" Sterling raised his voice. "I am fine and I will make my own decisions now."

He addressed the hospital staff, "Do not take orders from this man."

"Dad, please leave now. I've heard enough. You too Mom, I need to rest. I'll call the driver when I get released."

"Mr. and Mrs. Silver, I need to respect my patient's wishes. I must ask you to leave," the doctor said.

In the hallway, Mr. Silver took out his device and promptly sent a message to his contacts with children at his son's school.

It read, "Sterling is in the hospital. He broke up with his girlfriend today, and out of jealousy, it appears she pushed him into oncoming traffic. We aren't sure of the details yet. His injuries are serious. Please keep our family in your thoughts during this trying time"

"There," he thought, "that will serve her right." Mr. Silver hoped this desperate act would make Eden a pariah at school, then maybe she would leave and he could have his son back, his life back.

In his hospital bed, Sterling wished he could contact Eden. He needed to speak to her, but he was tired, so tired, and he fell back into sleep. When he woke, he saw through the window that it was dark. He called for the nurse.

"How long was I asleep?"

"Since Tuesday afternoon."

"What day is it now?"

"It's Friday night, 7pm."

"Has anyone been to see me?"

"No, the doctor ordered no visitors, not even your parents. He was following your wishes, and thought it best for your recovery."

"Did a girl come?" "No, no one since Tuesday. Well, except the old man, her grandfather I believe. He's just been sitting in the waiting room, but, come to think of it, I haven't seen him today."

Sterling was released the next morning. It was Saturday. He called for the driver to pick him up. He went straight to the entrance of the Inside, left his device in the car, and asked the driver to wait. The driver was distracted but could have sworn he saw the boy vanish into thin air by the old fence. He was not going to ask questions, his job was to drive the Silver family members as needed, nothing more. He'd witnessed some really interesting things working for the Silvers over the years, and he was skilled in the art of keeping his mouth shut.

Sterling found the burre Eden shared with her father and it was empty. As he stood there wondering what to do, a lady came out from another little burre and asked, "Are you looking for Mitch, because he's gone. He made his final exit last week on Tuesday morning."

"I never got to say goodbye." Sterling felt hot tears sting his eyes. He'd missed it and hadn't been there for Eden.

"Do you know where Eden is? I need to find her."

"No, she's been gone since Tuesday too, no one knows where she is."

Next Sterling went to the Sage who appeared deep in thought and distracted. The Sage said he hadn't seen Eden since they went to the hospital and he could not "see" where she was Outside.

Find Vita. She'll help you.

This was his only advice.

<u>27</u>

Death

When the Sage directed Sterling to find Vita, an image came to Sterling's mind immediately, of shelves crammed with dusty books and volumes. Vita was in Books. He thanked the Sage quickly and took off. Sterling approached and slowed his pace not wanting to burst in on Vita and startle her. People Inside moved slowly and quietly. Vita was on a sliding ladder arranging books on a topmost shelf, just as she'd appeared in his mind moments before.

"Sterling, you're here. Should you be? How are you?"

Vita backed down the ladder, faced him, and embraced him.

"Thank goodness you're okay. I've been so worried."

Then they simultaneously asked each other, "Do you know where Eden is?"

Vita spoke first, "I know she was going to Gemma's. She couldn't stay here alone, not after Mitch left. She said she felt helpless. Honestly, I thought she would come to you."

"No, she hasn't," Sterling said, his concern evident. "Not since Tuesday; then I was unconscious for three days. I don't know where Gemma lives, I've never been there."

"Close your eyes," Vita commanded, not sure this would work. "And quiet your mind."

Sterling obeyed, and once again, images flooded in. It was like watching a movie. He saw the streets, the train stops, the exact route to Gemma's. Next he saw inside the little apartment Gemma shared with her parents and her five siblings. He saw a large scruffy looking dog and two cats, one of which was sitting in the middle of the dining table on a pile of papers, and there was Eden in the midst of this family's chaos, her head thrown back in laughter, looking beautiful as ever, and happy.

"I see her, Vita. I see where she is. She looks so happy, so content there. I don't think I'll go to her. She's safe. I'll leave her alone."

Eden was happy. Gemma's home and family was a little haven of peace Outside. The family welcomed her. It was when they sat together to eat that Eden noticed the rings.

"Where did you get your rings?" she asked Gemma's parents.

"We got them from the Sage," Gemma's father said.

"Yes, we met Inside, and left together to become ambassadors. Once you cue in, you'll notice there are quite a few of us Outside. We signal the Sage if we find a Fallen who we think needs help." Eden looked at Gemma.

"Did you know this?"

"Yes."

Eden liked her even more and was thankful they'd become friends. It was nice having a friend who understood her, and there weren't many.

Eden hadn't been back to the hospital since visiting with the Sage. After the visit, she'd gone back Inside, gathered some clothing, and made her way to her friend's. It was too difficult to stay in the burre she had shared with her father, too soon to be there alone. She needed time to process Mitch's leaving and Sterling's injuries. She wanted to return to the hospital, but the truth was, she didn't trust herself around Sterling's father. The man was pure evil and the thoughts she had about him disturbed her. With the Sage present, she'd managed to control herself with great effort, but she didn't think it was possible if the man baited her again.

So, confident Sterling would find her when he was able, and if he chose to, she stayed away. Being at Gemma's had provided her the rest she needed to feel better. She had refused to see a doctor. Gemma stayed home with her. Monday, they returned to school together.

Walking down the halls at school, students parted and let her pass, and everything seemed normal enough, until Ember and her pack of nameless girlfriends sauntered up to Eden from behind. Eden read the thought and snide remarks before Ember ever spoke a word. Ember had been instrumental in spreading the rumor Mr. Silver created. It was a perfect opportunity for her to strike at Eden, her perceived enemy, from a cowardly distance. Ember's father had heard the news in a message from Sterling's father, and promptly forwarded it. Apparently Sterling broke up with his girlfriend and she'd pushed him into oncoming traffic causing a head injury, nearly killing him. The general opinion of the parents was that Eden should be expelled.

She only got into Upper School as a favor to her father, and by the way, he's not really her biological father. The only reason she hasn't been expelled immediately is because the administration is taking pity on her since her father just died, poor girl.

So the story, or some version of it, went.

It was the most anyone had ever communicated with each other. Messages were flying, and it seemed everyone was in on the conversation through their devices.

"This is why Commoners should never be allowed at U.S.A. They are nothing but trouble."

"We need to protect our own."

"The school's reputation will suffer."

It seemed parents and students alike were united in their smugness and self-entitlement and common dislike for those beneath them. Eden was a perfect target.

Eden turned around and her eyes met Ember's. Ember was thrown back by a force only she felt. Once again her face swelled with angry welts and pustules and to her dismay, she discovered that her legs were too weak to stand and run.

"That's the poison releasing itself," Eden said. She spun on her heel and walked away.

"Help me," Ember commanded her group of girlfriends, but they were backing away. No one wanted to touch her. They feared she might be contagious.

"Help me, help me!" Ember screamed desperately.

Only Gemma offered a hand, and escorted Ember to the office. No words passed between them. The remainder of the school day was uneventful. Eden's plan was to go to Gemma's house again. She was still not ready to go home. She wondered what "home" would be without her father. Gemma's parents had invited her to stay with them for as long as she needed or wanted, and she knew they were completely sincere.

When school finished, Eden found Vita waiting at the front of the campus. How odd it was to see her there in her beige tunic, her chestnut hair, wild. She looked so out of place. It was strange and humbling. Eden knew the courage it must have taken for Vita to venture out, especially alone. She didn't even have the Sage with her. Eden hugged her close.

"How did you get here? Are you okay? This is Gemma, the friend I told you about."

"I'm fine. Really. I needed to see you. Hi, Gemma, it's nice to meet you."

"You too," Gemma held out her hand to Vita, but they hugged instead.

"I came because I needed to see you, to talk to you, and this was the only way. It's Sterling. You should go to him. You need to go to him. He came Inside looking for you. He's really angry with his father, and there's something you should know."

Eden wasn't sure how to put her thoughts into words, but she tried.

"Look, um, I think Sterling might be better off without me. I've caused a lot of trouble for him, especially with his father. Besides, he knows how to find me... if he wants to."

"Oh Eden, can't you see? He feels like you're better off without him, that he's the one who's caused you grief. Am I the only one who knows you two need each other? You belong together. I don't know why you're doubting it now," Vita said.

"No, you're not the only one who knows it. They do need each other. I completely agree," Gemma added.

Eden felt as if a temporary fog cleared. She hadn't been herself since the accident, the confrontation with Mr. Silver, and then her beloved father leaving; it was all so much to process.

"You're right, both of you," she said as the realization dawned upon her.

"There's something else," Vita said, "I think Sterling is the 'bright angel' from the prophecy, but I don't think he knows it yet."

At first it seemed shocking, impossible to Eden, but suddenly it all made sense, and she knew she must get to Sterling immediately. If he found out what his father had done to her, the threats, the rumor, his plan to destroy her, Eden was afraid of what Sterling would do, and it would be her fault. She was the reason.

"I need to go to him right now," Eden told her friends and she ran to catch the next train. There was no time to explain the vision that came clearly to her mind.

The journey to Sterling's did nothing to quell Eden's anxiety. She couldn't get there fast enough. She got off at the exit and ran the entire way, her head throbbing. She didn't have a nose guard and was breathing the poison air. At the entrance, the guard paused, he'd been warned by Mr. Silver, she was not allowed in the compound, but before he could speak, Eden looked at him. Her eyes communicated the message quite clearly. The guard let her pass.

Eden put the code in at Sterling's front door and closed it quietly behind her. She knew she'd find Sterling and Mr. Silver in his office. The vision was quite clear. She opened the door and there they were, father and son. Good, she wasn't too late. Mr. Silver exploded with rage when he saw her.

"You are not welcome here. How did you get in? You are an intruder, and I could kill you right now with no consequence."

That is exactly what he intended to do as he reached for his hand gun in the open desk drawer. And what Sterling intended to do was prevent it in the only way possible. He would have to kill his father to keep Eden safe. He knew it. Eden knew it too. Sterling lunged for his father planning to choke him with his bare hands. Eden would not allow it. She stepped between them. She touched Mr. Silver on his arm. The paralysis started. It spread up his arm.

"What did you do?" he spat, "I knew you were evil."

Then to his son, "Sterling, she's evil. It's not too late. Stop her."

Then he took a pathetic, submissive tone and resorted to begging.

"I'm sorry, Son, I won't hurt her. I promise. Please, please make it stop."

Within minutes he fell to the floor unable to stand, unable to speak, the paralysis taking over his body and shutting it down. Eden and Sterling stood and watched in disbelief as the man turned to ash, a fine black dust, till there was nothing but a tiny pile. Eden walked over and opened the window. The dust was swept up in the breeze and sucked out of the room into the air.

Eden wanted badly to stay there, in the moment, forever with Sterling. He held her tight against him and stroked her hair.

"Eden I need to be Inside," Sterling said. "And I want you with me. We can go together. We'll always be safe. It's what's right." But even as he said it, he 'saw' it wouldn't happen. It wasn't to be.

"I know," Eden replied. "But I can't. I'm the dark force. What your father said is true. He was evil, but so am I. You aren't. You are the light. I can't be with you. I have to say good-bye. It's the only way."

"I love you, Eden. I don't think I'll ever love anyone else."

"You will, Sterling. I know you will. I love you too, but I have to leave. I have to."

It was then they noticed the Sage was there in the room.

You don't have to do this alone, Eden. I'm here.

Eden let go of Sterling and stepped away. She went to the Sage. He held out his arms and she folded into them. She closed her eyes and focused all her power inward. It took only seconds. They were bathed in white light and were gone. There was no darkness.

Sterling was overcome, overwhelmed. When he finally uncurled himself from a ball on the floor, he saw a second ring on his finger.

28

The Sage

Sterling was in a daze, his new role weighing heavily upon him. He didn't want the responsibility of the Sage, but knew now it was his alone. He felt no different and was halfway expecting divine intervention to inspire him. None came. He moved freely from one world to the next and as he did, people seemed naturally drawn to him. There was a time, ages ago it felt, that this would have brought nothing but revulsion. He'd never liked people generally, even when he was a small child. With each day his tolerance grew, and as he opened his mind, the data trickled in.

A man would approach and in an instant Sterling knew him, wholly knew him, his thoughts, anxieties, flaws and strengths. Sterling remembered that the previous Sage had resided Inside and was rarely seen Outside. Sterling's contact with the Sage had been limited and he strained to recall every personal interaction and any information Eden had given him. The pain of losing her was still raw and he wondered if it was possible he'd ever get over it.

The easiest plan would be to end his life, but he knew he wouldn't join her if he did, or even if he could, as the new Sage. What he did know was that no one who ends their life on purpose can ever move forward and he was certain Eden had moved forward. Sometimes as he walked he caught a scent of her. It was sunshine and pine, warm and soothing, just right. When this happened, he wanted time to stop or suspend it while he breathed in and remembered.

The Sage will walk among you and be one of you, and he will help you find your way forward.

Sterling wasn't sure he was up to the task.

He came upon the hollowed out log, the one with the perfect place to sit, the place where Mitch had met the Sage years before, where he and Eden used to sit and talk for hours. It was a comfortable place, conforming to whoever's body was in it, a thinking place, a place of peace. The old Sage always seemed to just know what people needed, who should come Inside, and who was ready to exit. He'd been a quiet presence. Sterling felt like he was going about the role all wrong. *What did it take to lead?* There was no instruction manual.

He decided to sit awhile, close his eyes, and meditate. Soon he could feel someone else sit down and he hesitated to open his eyes. He knew the person wouldn't leave, he felt her patience. She was waiting for him. She smelled like Eden and he wanted to enjoy the scent and imagine it was his best friend next to him before he opened his eyes to reality.

When he finally looked, he recognized the lady immediately as a former Fallen. She'd left to work with children in the Exit Ceremony he'd witnessed with Eden years ago. He couldn't read her full story and he wondered how she was back Inside.

He began with, "Hello".

"I was hoping to find you, Sage," she said.

"How do you know I'm the Sage?"

"We all know. We knew from the minute you took over. And Mitch told some of us just before he left."

"Are you shocked? I'm sure I hardly seem the type."

"Oh, is there a type? I doubt it." The woman was friendly and Sterling felt comfortable speaking with her. He felt okay to ask, "Weren't you a Fallen? I feel I recognize you from about five or six years ago at your Exit Ceremony."

"Yes, same person. My name is Serene. I'm married to Drake, you may have met him. He lived here for a year or so. We met Outside, after we exited. We both worked at Abandoned Children, trying to save the world, you know."

Sterling was curious and had to ask.

"I don't understand how you're back Inside. How did you do it?"

It was then he noticed the bundle she was carrying close to her chest. It started to stir and there was a little sound. A baby?

Serene explained, "Drake and I wanted a child so badly, but hardly anyone has children anymore. It's so rare. I figured

I'd have to be content with caring for the ones at the center. Then last week a baby was dropped off. We don't know by whom. The camera didn't capture the person and it was clear he, or she, did not want to be seen. From the minute I picked the baby up, I knew she'd be ours and I also knew I wanted to bring her Inside.

I wanted her to grow up here. I know the rules, but thought I'd try. I just walked in, I got through, and since then I've been looking for you to ask if it's okay, if I need some sort of permission or something in order to stay."

"No permission needed." Sterling recalled the first prophecy he'd received as Sage, which now made more sense.

There will be less division between Inside and Outside. The worlds must function together. The Inside can spread and heal the Outside.

"Can I see her?" Sterling asked.

The proud mom gingerly handed over the bundle. Pine and sunshine and fresh air and warmth hit him all at once. Sterling looked down at the baby. He reached to touch her face. She grabbed his finger with her tiny, perfect hand and gazed up at him with violet eyes.

"We haven't named her, yet."

"Her name is Eden," the new Sage said.

About the author

Deanna Nese is the author of two other novels.

Shelter in Place (2014) is a contemporary Christian fiction tale of three women coming together to help a young mother raise her child.

Yellow Slicker (2022) is a psychological thriller about Duncan's deepest, darkest secret and someone else finding out about it.

The Needle's Eye was originally published in 2016 with iUniverse.

Her short story, Frank's Reviews was published by Typishly in 2018. Her flash fiction has been published in the VC Reporter. She teaches middle school students English Literature, Writing, and History. She enjoys outdoor activities, reading, and writing in all genres, as well as spending time with her family. Deanna is also a member of the Crime Writers Association (CWA).